INTO THE
WINDWRACKED WILDS

AS A. DEBORAH BAKER

Over the Woodward Wall
Along the Saltwise Sea
Into the Windwracked Wilds

AS SEANAN McGUIRE

Middlegame
Seasonal Fears
Dusk or Dark or Dawn or Day
Deadlands: Boneyard
Dying With Her Cheer Pants On
Laughter at the Academy

THE WAYWARD CHILDREN SERIES

Every Heart a Doorway
Down Among the Sticks and Bones
Beneath the Sugar Sky
In an Absent Dream
Come Tumbling Down
Across the Green Grass Fields
Where the Drowned Girls Go
Seanan McGuire's Wayward Children,
Volumes 1–3 (boxed set)

THE OCTOBER DAYE SERIES

Rosemary and Rue
A Local Habitation
An Artificial Night
Late Eclipses
One Salt Sea
Ashes of Honor
Chimes at Midnight
The Winter Long

A Red-Rose Chain
Once Broken Faith
The Brightest Fell
Night and Silence
The Unkindest Tide
A Killing Frost
When Sorrows Come
Be the Serpent

A TOM DOHERTY ASSOCIATES BOOK

New York

INTO THE WINDWRACKED WILDS

A. Deborah Baker

INTO THE WINDWRACKED WILDS

Copyright © 2022 by Seanan McGuire

A Tordotcom Book
Published by Tom Doherty Associates
120 Broadway
New York, NY 10271

www.tor.com

Tor® is a registered trademark of Macmillan Publishing Group, LLC.

Library of Congress Cataloging-in-Publication Data

Names: Baker, A. Deborah, author.
Title: Into the windwracked wilds / A. Deborah Baker.
Description: First edition. | New York : Tom Doherty Associates, 2022. | Series: The up-and-under ; 3
Identifiers: LCCN 2022019345 (print) | LCCN 2022019346 (ebook) | ISBN 9781250848444 (hardcover) | ISBN 9781250848437 (ebook)
Subjects: LCGFT: Fantasy fiction.
Classification: LCC PS3607.R36395 I59 2022 (print) | LCC PS3607.R36395 (ebook) | DDC 813/.6—dc23/eng/20220420
LC record available at https://lccn.loc.gov/2022019345
LC ebook record available at https://lccn.loc.gov/2022019346

Our books may be purchased in bulk for promotional, educational, or business use. Please contact your local bookseller or the Macmillan Corporate and Premium Sales Department at 1-800-221-7945, extension 5442, or by email at MacmillanSpecialMarkets@macmillan.com.

First Edition: 2022

Printed in the United States of America

0 9 8 7 6 5 4 3 2 1

FOR MAC AND SCOUT.
WHAT ADVENTURES YOU HAVE
WAITING FOR YOU.
WHAT MYSTERIES TO UNCOVER,
WHAT MOUNTAINS TO CLIMB.

I CAN'T WAIT TO WATCH.

INTO THE
WINDWRACKED WILDS

ONE

REMINDERS AND DEFINITIONS

We have left the territory of once upon a time at this point. Once upon a time is for the beginning of stories, and we are now well and truly mired in the sticky, unpredictable middle. There is a commonality to beginnings. We meet people; we learn their names and the sketches of their stories; we see the situation beginning to unfold in front of them; we either decide we're interested enough to follow them over the woodward wall or down the road of glistening nacre, like the trail of some fairy-kissed snail slithering through a world of impossible things, or we turn back and let them be. Not every story is for every person, you see, and if a tale baits its hook and dangles it in front of us and we feel no temptation to bite, there is no shame in walking away. There are many fish in the sea. There are many hooks as well.

If you are still here with me now, then when the scrimshaw hook etched with the names "Avery" and "Zib" was dangled in front of you, you were happy to slide it between your lips and into the space between your cheek and your teeth. You bit down, and have since been pulled out of the shallows and safe harbor of once upon a time, and now swim the choppy seas of the middle of the story with the rest of us. I am not sorry. I am glad, in fact, that you are here, for stories cannot be nothing but beginnings: they must have a vast and terrible middle to get them from hook to home. Thank you for allowing me to catch you. We have so far left to go.

But as the beginning is some distance behind us now, it seems proper for me to remind you, at least a little, of where we are going and how we have reached this point. I promise I will not take long, as the story itself is on the other side of this digression, and we would all prefer to get there quickly.

So: once, long enough ago that your parents were not there, but recently enough that the world had things like schools and indoor plumbing and telephones, there were two children living on the same street, by the names of Avery Alexander Grey and Hepzibah Laurel Jones. Avery's parents were disgusted by the idea of nicknames, and only ever called him "Avery," as if he had yet to earn the rest of the name for his own use. Hepzibah's parents, on the other hand, thought a name was like a shirt or a sweater, and needed to be bigger than the child, so they could grow into it as they figured out the person they were going to be. And so they called their daughter "Zib" to the point where some people thought that was her own and only given name, and she never once minded the truncation.

Avery and Zib were not friends when they shared that street, that town, that world; they were close together according to the map, but very far apart according to the world, which sometimes bears no resemblance to lines on paper. They lived separate if parallel lives, and could have happily gone on that way until they left the shallows of their childhood and bit down on the bitter hook of adulthood, which would pull them into a much deeper sea.

It was perhaps coincidence and perhaps contrivance and most likely some alchemy made by combining the two that a water main burst one morning as both of them readied themselves for school, and they found their morning walk directed down a new and unfamiliar path. And as they walked, they each found themselves confronted with a new and unfamiliar person: the other. They might each have dismissed the strange child—for they were deeply strange to one another's eyes, Avery with his perfectly shined shoes, Zib with her mended skirt and wild, uncombed hair—and gone out without remembering them at all, had the sidewalk not come to an end at a wall that should not have been there, and on the wall's other side, a forest that should not have been there either.

What they found on the other side of the wall is the territory of "once," and we have already been there, have explored and understood that landscape, made it our own to the best of our abilities. We are welcome to revisit it whenever the need strikes, but we have no need to make such a visit now. So we will only wave to those distant and dwindled versions of the people we know, people who have never met a girl who is also a murder of crows, or a bear who is also a hive of bees, or a road with opinions about its own destination. How strange they seem to us now, how very queer! We have moved so far beyond them that they might as well be strangers, for all that we were with them at the start. We must continue on.

After "once" comes "upon," and the children found themselves uneasy companions in a strange new world, walking a rainbow road that bent and twisted at its own whim, charting its own course across the map. At one end, the Impossible City, where all good things were locked behind gleaming mother-of-pearl walls, where a way home might be found by eager children who were willing to work for what they wanted. At the other end, somewhere in the vast unknown, the Queen of Wands, ruler of this patchwork land, without whom no journey could ever be completed. And in the middle, the Saltwise

Sea, domain of pirates and princesses, sailors and serpents, where even the waves have opinions about the way things are going to go.

The beginning was simpler, of that there could be no question. But the children had entered the middle, and so they had to navigate that sea, until they found themselves turning back toward the shore, following the improbable road wherever it wished to go.

From "upon" we find our way to "a," which is the shortest and simplest of the words we have to travel through. It is a letter, without which many words fall into nonsensical disrepair. It is an article, recontextualizing everything after. *A* city is different from *the* city is different from *any* city. The Impossible City is the only exemplar of its kind, and as such receives the vaunted "the," rather than the generous "a." To say something happened "once upon time" is to say nothing at all or, if we are being very generous, that something happened at all times, but only once. Once, a babe was born wrapped in a name that never fit quite right, like a cloak of feathers sized to someone else. And once, that babe's heart was broken so completely the shards could never be put back together.

Once, that babe became a girl, not yet quite a woman, but sliding down that seemingly inevitable road, like a balloon on a string being pulled from one end of her own lifetime to the next. Once, the woman that girl was becoming revolted, and cried, from the secret eggshell palace of her very self, "No. I will not become what you would make of me; I am already a heartless thing because of what has been done without my consent, I will not be a person you define by the character of the heart I do not have." Once, that girl walked the impossible road on her own, and had her own adventures, as so many children had done before her and still more would do after her. Once, her adulthood caught up to her, and she had no choice but to sit and be still and quiet, to be biddable as the people who controlled such things asked for her to be.

Once, she rose from her place, threw aside her burdens, and went to a woman who called herself a queen for no reason other than that the winds—one of the four pillars that held their world up to the sky—loved her better than they loved anyone else. Once, the woman knelt before the queen, shed her raiment and her rationality, and asked to be made something that would have no need for weeping.

Once, the Queen of Swords ripped out the woman's burning ember of a heart, held it in her hand, and crumpled it to ashes for the winds to scatter to the four corners of the world, to earth and sea and flaming field, and remade that babe in the image of a murder, black-winged and heartless and free as any sky. Once, the woman was no more, had no name, but was a Crow Girl, monstrous and perfect and wild, and once, all these things were true, and once, they were better left forgotten.

So you see, the events we follow here and now, on the long and rainbowed ribbon of the improbable road, depend upon the "a" even more than they depend upon "once." They are not singular events in their shape, but only in their order, which assembles here for the first time in history. Our Avery, our Zib, their cool and clever companions, they are a first, and they follow the improbable road as have so many before them, seeking answers more than they seek adventure, but finding adventure all the same.

When first they found the improbable road, it reached across fields and farmlands, extending from and to a great city, and these were normal things for a road to do, not so improbable at all. But as they continued on, the road found new places to root itself, and they found themselves walking on beaches, through briars, and on the surface of the ocean itself.

As we leave the concluded certainty of "upon" for the fresh new surprises of "a," we step back into the purview of time itself, which has been happening all through this sweet digression, this brief attempt to delay the inevitable arrival of the future. Time will always catch up with you, in the end. There are some who would call it a fifth element, a side effect of aether, as smoke is a side effect of flame. Without time, everything would happen at once, and be finished so quickly that there would be no chance for storytelling, or for children, or for improbable roads to exist at all. Time is the most essential of the elements of this tale.

And so, with time once more firmly in our pocket, we join our brave companions walking on the water, the improbable road wrapping itself around waves like a vine around a tree, as firm and stable beneath the feet of the four children as any solid ground. The road held them up, safe from the depths, time flowed around them, and the children walked on.

TWO

FOLLOWING THE
IMPROBABLE ROAD

Zib led the way across the waves, her untamable curls dampened with sea spray and her clothes soaked with salt water. If this bothered her at all, she gave no indication, and she walked as gleefully barefoot as she ever had. The road beneath their feet was dry and steady, having no interest in shaking them off or allowing them to slip and fall into the roiling waters of the Saltwise Sea.

Behind her walked Avery, closer to the center of the road, which was an easy six feet across. He could remain mostly dry if he stayed there, although occasionally a playful wave broke against the road's edge to dampen his feet. They had all been wearing iron shoes when they set out on the road, shod in the earth's hard, unrelenting heart, and while the shoes had been surprisingly comfortable for something smelted on a forge, they had also been heavy. For the first time in his life, Avery was barefoot because he wanted to be, having pushed his iron shoes over the road's edge some time before, watching them sink with a feeling that was caught somewhere between curiosity and satisfaction.

There is no name for that feeling, which is almost entirely the purview of cats and children. Cats have little interest in the naming of transitory things, and children, while they name anything and everything around them, all too often do so in the secret language of the very young, which slips away from them like mist as they age.

Growing up is a process of exchanges. Not always fair ones, but exchanges all the same. We trade sturdiness away to grow taller and farther from the ground, so that falling hurts more; we trade the language of the wind and trees, the runic writing of the sunbeams, for better understanding of the world the adults have made between themselves, joining the great consensus that began so long before any one of us, and will of necessity endure when all of us who walk our own improbable roads now are gone. Avery had not yet quite lost the space between curiosity and satisfaction, but it would leave him soon, and when it did, it would never come back again.

Behind Avery walked a girl who took each step

as if she were unsure about the very notion of stepping, as if to walk were a strange and terrible new
experience, and one she still wasn't sure she enjoyed.
Seagulls wheeled overhead, wings white against
the cloudless sky, and the looks they gave her were
pointedly unfriendly. She shivered and kept walking.
Her hair was black and her dress matched it, made of
pitch-colored feathers slicked down by salt water. It
stuck to her body, not impeding her freedom to keep
following the road. She looked constantly from side
to side as she walked, head moving in short, sharp
bursts, as if she were afraid of somehow missing the
adventure getting underway, as if she didn't have
enough eyes to see everything that mattered.

After her came the last but not the least of them,
in appearance the youngest of the four, a little shorter
than Avery and a little slighter than Zib, with very
pale skin that lacked the healthiness of someone who
is pale because they spend a lot of time indoors reading books and avoiding the sun, or because their
parents have been very, very good about encourag-
ing them to wear sunscreen. Instead, her skin had
the faintly white-blue undertone of someone who
has fallen into a lake and drowned, and it glittered
with silver specks, like a dusting of the smallest fish
scales in the entire world. Her hair was so wet that
it hung from her head in long, straight locks like
waterweeds. Water dripped from it, trickling along
the length of her body to puddle on the road. That

was why she came last. She created a slipping hazard for the other three.

Zib paused, and the rest of them paused as well, as they had learned to do after a few accidental collisions. No one had yet fallen off the road by accident—the damp and dripping girl at the back of their line had stepped off it a few times, to walk along the surface of the sea like it was nothing at all to do so—but they were all too aware of how deep the water was beneath them, and how easy it would be to overbalance and go tumbling down into the depths.

"Do you see something?" asked Avery. He hated the hunger in his own voice, the sheer raw need to be back on solid ground, but it was there, and it would have done him no good at all to deny it.

We are all elemental creatures, in one way or another, and what flexibility we take from that reality is spent early—even earlier than the space between curiosity and satisfaction, which lingers as long as it likes, often long past the point where a child has settled into whatever element will best serve them. And some people find their elements early, only to change them later in life for something that fits them a little better. Niamh, the drowned girl, who must be named at some point, even in a story that has ridden all the way from "once" to "time," was a child of water. She might not have been, before she had drowned, might have been a bright and burning fire-bird girl, or a wild and wistful daughter of the air, but "might have been" and "maybe" are countries that can only ever be visited, and never lived in. Niamh was a drowned girl, all the way to the waterlogged bottom of her bones, and she had never been more comfortable than she was when she walked upon the Saltwise Sea.

Avery, in contrast, was as deeply rooted a creature of earth as he could possibly have been without being in some way made of stone or soil or growing green. He believed things had shapes and shapes had a purpose, and however much he was shown that sometimes, in places like the Up-and-Under— for that was the name of the world traveled by the improbable road, where the rules of all things were slightly different than the rules Avery and Zib had known at home—things could change themselves, he continued to cling stubbornly to the truths he knew in the secret chambers of his stationary heart. A thing had a shape, and it should cleave to that shape whenever it possibly could.

The Saltwise Sea was thus something of an offense to his way of looking at the world, as were all oceans, for the shape of an ocean is a fluctuating one, never the same between one breath and the next. Parts of them may freeze, but never all the way to the deepest depths, where the dark fish swim and the secret caverns dream. (If these are things that do not sing to you, do not worry. They will be known in their time, and carry no more importance in this tale than the span of this digression, which is finished now.) Parts of them may dry, or draw back from the shore for a time, but the oceans will always return. This is their promise. This is their threat.

For Avery, walking on a road stretched across the surface of the sea like the skin of a peach, and equally as fragile, was a labor beyond all undertaking. He was more than ready to be back on solid ground, where he could trust that an errant wave would never sweep in and carry him away. Where he could find a fresh pair of shoes, for even as Zib preferred to be barefoot at all times and under all circumstances, he despised the feeling of the world beneath his feet, and wanted nothing but good, honest socks and shoes against his toes. So when Zib stopped walking, he felt hope blossom in his chest like a terrible flower, dressed in thorns and ready to do him harm.

As for Zib, she shook her head, lips drawn down in a petulant pout, and said, "I don't know, really. It seems like the water goes on forever. Niamh? Do you know where we are?"

"I could, if you wanted me to," said Niamh. She looked at the edge of the road with a light and a hunger in her eyes, like a rabbit considering the tangled edge of a thorn brake, or a hawk considering the sheer drop-off of a high cliff. "Do you want me to?"

Surprisingly, the response came not from Zib or Avery, but from the Crow Girl, who wrapped her arms around her salt-sodden dress of feathers, and said, in a voice sharp as a summons, "Yes. Yes, we want you to. Yes, *I* want you to. Go, and find out, and come back, and tell us."

"Are you all right?" asked Avery, who had been so uncomfortable with his own distance from the land that he had been paying less attention to the Crow Girl's unhappiness than he should have been.

"Any one of these bad birds could be in the service of the Page of Ceaseless Storms," snapped the Crow Girl. "I can't break myself into pieces, as I'm meant to be, and share the skies with them, or they harass and harry and pluck my feathers and try to drive me to the water, where I'll drown and they won't. If enough pieces of me die, I'll die too, and you know that as well as you know anything, because I've told it to you before! So I have to stay all one *stupid* shape, like I'm a girl all the time and not a murder at all, and I'm afraid I'll forget how to be crows if I don't go back to them soon. I hate this ocean, and I hate this place, and I hate this stupid, *stupid* road."

And she stomped her bare foot on the improbable road, and it winked out like a soap bubble, and all four of them were unceremoniously dumped into the water without even so much as a splash.

THREE

DROWNING AS A COMMUNITY ENRICHMENT ACTIVITY

Four children, suddenly deprived of the same road, dropped into the same ocean, will sink at different rates for many reasons.

Zib, for all that her hair was damp, was wearing a longer skirt and a heavier sweater than any of the rest of them, and her dampened hair was still full of curls and snarls that trapped and held bubbles of air. Once she was properly waterlogged, all those things would become weight to drag her down, but in the very first instants, they provided the buoyancy she needed to stay at least a little bit afloat, sinking slowly into the blue.

The Crow Girl sank even more slowly, being a creature of air and empty spaces, from her hollow bones to her hollow heart. If not for the water already weighing down her feathers, she might not have sunk at all, but bobbed up to the surface like a bit of debris, pushed back and forth by the waves, remaining upright and unsubmerged.

Niamh, daughter of water, didn't sink at all. When the road vanished and she dropped with the rest, the momentum of her fall drove her beneath the surface, and for a moment she simply hung there, wide-eyed and surprised by the sudden absence of anything beneath her feet. Then she shook her head, blinking the water from her eyes, and swam after Zib as she sank, trying to reach the other girl before she went too far.

There was no reaching Avery. He was the densest of them, being made entirely of solid, practical things, like bones and muscles and determination to do whatever anyone could ask of him, and he sank like the stone he sometimes wished he was, trailing bubbles behind himself. He sank without thrashing for the first few seconds, almost too surprised to understand what was going on. Then he began to flail, fighting against gravity and density and the currents of the Saltwise Sea, trying to make his way back to the surface.

He could never have made it there in time. Even had he been able to get his bearings and swim back up to the air, he would have been too slow. Their drop into the water had happened without warning, and there was no world where he could have saved himself without sacrificing his friends at the same time. But still he tried, animal instinct and human panic uniting for one of those rare, perfect moments of consensus. Avery wanted to live. Whatever that meant, he wanted it, and he wanted it badly enough to fight for it.

Of the four of them, he was the one who thrashed the hardest, and perhaps that was what sent ripples echoing through the open sea, tiny tendrils of presence that resonated into depths none of them, not even Niamh, would live to see. And the Saltwise Sea, which was called "wise" both to indicate its location on the map and the character of its currents, heard them. It heard the cries of children in distress, and as so many oceans would not, it responded.

From the depths rose a great, pointed shape, long as a fish and sinuous as an eel, both dark and light at the same time, depending on the angle of its bullet-shaped body; its fins were spaced like a seal's, and its tail was long and sweeping, fringed with fins. It rose swiftly, cutting through the water like a blade, and as it drew nearer to the sinking children, it opened its mouth, revealing a long cavern lined with short, jagged teeth. Zib, looking down as she sank, was the first to notice it.

She began to fight against the water, trying to pull herself away from the enormous, swiftly approaching predator. Even in the very best and brightest of worlds, she could never have been faster than the creature, which rose like an arrow streaking toward its target, inevitable and inescapable. Still, she tried, and perhaps it was her reward that she was the first one it reached, mouth gaping wider still as it swallowed her whole.

Cornering in the water like there had never been an easier thing to do, the creature swam for the thrashing Avery, gulping him down as easily as it had taken Zib. The Crow Girl was next, and she broke into birds as she passed the outline of its jaws, dozens of smaller, feathered creatures appearing where one seemingly human girl had been, and disappearing just as quickly.

Of the four, only Niamh didn't thrash, or try to swim away. She looked at the great shape in the water as it turned toward her, and she stopped moving, and she spread her arms, and she smiled as it swallowed her, the motion of its throat carrying her into the deep darkness of its gullet.

The mouth was a narrow channel filled with teeth and rushing water and a few unlucky fish that had been too slow to flee from the chaos the children created. Niamh hugged her body and made herself as small as possible, like she was a pill to ease an unhappy stomach or stop an aching head, and the great muscular surface of the creature's tongue pulsed beneath her, pushing her to the back of its throat, until she was sliding along a long channel, past the tight-sealed veil of its larynx, down the pulsing tube of its esophagus. Still, she hugged herself, and the walls of the creature's throat pulled her ever deeper down. The water drained away, falling faster than she did, until she was inexplicably surrounded by air, strangely sweet even here in the literal belly of the beast.

At the bottom of the throat, with one last muscular contraction, the esophagus spat her free, into a dark, oddly cavernous room. She landed on her bottom in a shallow pool of water, maybe half a foot deep, and blinked as she looked around herself, seeing nothing. Not that she had expected to, necessarily; she was inside a sea monster, after all, and it only followed that it would be too dark to see.

Darkness is not the same as silence. Pushing herself to her feet, she cupped her hands around her mouth, and called, "Is anyone else here?"

Rustling answered her, and then a series of caws from all directions, sharp and staccato and distressed. Niamh sighed.

"I don't speak the language of crows," she said. "I'm a Drowned Girl, not a Jackdaw, and the only birds I can translate for are cormorants and Swan Princesses. If you were a Swan Princess, you wouldn't sound nearly so unhappy. You'd be too busy making other people sound that way."

The crows called again, louder and angrier. Niamh scowled into the dark.

"Well, I can't understand you, so you're going to have to be a girl again if you want to have a conversation."

More caws.

"Is it too dark? Is that why you're upset?" Maybe the Crow Girl couldn't find all the disassembled parts of herself in the darkness of the creature's belly.

This time, the answering caws were barely shy of sullen, the resentful reply of a girl who had suddenly found herself isolated from the majority of herself.

Niamh sighed again. "I'll help as I can, but I'm not sure I can do anything," she said. "All my body's magic has gone into keeping me alive in your horrid dry world, and not to making light to make things easier for someone who's careless enough to let herself be scattered into crows."

A crow replied, voice harsh, and Niamh moved toward the sound, holding out her hand until her fingers brushed feathers, and then staying still until the creature could step onto her.

"So you know, I'm expecting you to come back together as soon as you have enough of yourself to survive as a girl," she said, voice stern. "I refuse to carry all of you just because you got your feathers wet and you don't want to do the work."

The crow hiccupped a meek reply, and Niamh began feeling her way into the dark, listening for the rustle of feathers and the croak of crows. She had

never seen the Crow Girl break into more than fifty
birds at once, which was still far too many birds to
be looking for in the belly of a sea monster. But she
had been speaking in a normal voice, and hadn't
heard anything from either Avery or Zib; maybe they
were somewhere else inside the beast, and the best
thing for her to do now was to make herself useful.

Gathering crows until she got her friend back and
could have a reasonable conversation with another
person was quite useful enough for her. And so she
kept moving, not letting herself think about the
other possible reasons for the silence of her friends.

Deeper inside the creature, Avery rolled onto his
back and stared upward at the blank nothingness that
his eyesight allowed. Then he coughed, sitting halfway upright as he tried to expel the water from his
lungs. The more water he spat out, the more water it
seemed like there was to spit, until he was bent dou-
ble, hacking and straining, and finally vomited a great
salty gout of water onto the surface beneath him.

He couldn't call it a "floor," exactly; "floor" implied someone had come along with a hammer and
nails and created something where nothing had been
before. And he couldn't call it "ground," because
ground didn't pulse under your hands like a thing
living, slick and firm and warmer than he would ever
have expected. So he didn't know what it was, and
thinking about what it *wasn't* seemed less complicated than facing the fact that something huge and

terrifying and unfamiliar had swallowed him the way a frog might swallow a fly.

Some people are very good indeed at not thinking about the way the world really is, or seeing the things that are really happening around them. This is called "denial." Avery was not one of those people. He did his best to refuse the things he didn't want the world to do or be or inflict upon him, but he always seemed to fail. And so the sound of a voice coming through the darkness was the most welcome thing he had ever heard.

"Avery?" The voice was Zib's, more familiar and more well-loved by the day. "Is that you?"

Avery scrambled to his feet. "It ate you, too?" Because that was the last thing he had seen before the whole world went dark: the teeth of some vast and awful *thing*, reaching up from the depths of the ocean to swallow him whole. For the first time, it occurred to him to maybe be a little bit glad that he had been eaten by something so *large*. Anything smaller would have needed to chew first, and then he wouldn't be having this conversation at all. Maybe it was a good thing to be swallowed by something so much bigger than yourself that it barely even noticed you were there.

Really, their entire time in the Up-and-Under had been like this beast, coming out of nowhere and gulping them down into the dark without so much as a by-your-leave.

"It did," Zib confirmed. She sounded closer now. "I think it was a mosasaur. I have pictures of them in one of my books, and what I saw looked a whole lot like one of those. Not real pictures, though. Drawing pictures, like you make with paint or chalk. Nobody has real pictures of a mosasaur."

"Why not?"

"Because there aren't any mosasaurs anymore. They were alive when the dinosaurs were alive, and they all died a long, long time ago, when the big volcano went off and killed all their food. Mosasaurs lived in the water, so I don't guess they were too bothered by the smoke, but they were so big they had to eat dinosaurs to feel full, and when all the dinosaurs died, the mosasaurs died too."

Something about that didn't sound quite right to Avery, but Zib was the one who knew what the thing that had eaten them was called, and that probably meant she knew the rest of what she was saying. And there wasn't any point in arguing when they were inside something.

"Are you all right?" he asked, anxious as ever.

"Wet, but yeah, otherwise I'm good. I got a little banged around when it swallowed me up, but now I'm fine. Keep talking. It's helping me find you in here."

"What do you want me to talk about?"

"I don't know. Whatever. Um. What you hope we'll find when we reach the end of the ocean. Were we even walking toward the beach?"

"Gosh, I hope so." Avery didn't know exactly what the difference was between an ocean and a lake, but he was pretty sure it was size. He'd tried to swim across the lake behind his family's summer home once, and he hadn't even made it halfway across before he'd been too tired to keep going. For a long, horrible moment he'd expected to drown in the lake and sink to the bottom, where his parents would never find his bones, tangled up among the waterweeds and turned into palaces for fishes.

If that was how big a lake was, how big did something have to be before people would call it an ocean and act like it was important enough to have queens and cities and sailing ships? Bigger than he could imagine. If they hadn't turned back toward the beach, if the improbable road had been leading them out to sea, then they were never going to be able to walk the whole way before they got too tired, or too hungry, or too thirsty to keep going. It was odd to be thirsty when there was water everywhere in every direction, but salt water didn't make things any better, and it had been a long time since the orange juice on the Lady's ship.

He'd never really expected to miss the ship. He'd also never expected to be following a road that had opinions about things much of anywhere, much less across the surface of the sea. Avery was coming to learn that what he expected and what the world wanted to do often bore no real resemblance to one another.

"Maybe we weren't and we'll wind up on a whole new continent!"

Zib sounded very close now. Avery almost thought he could reach out and touch her, and so he tried, smiling to himself when his fingers found the wet, matted shape of her hair, which was already dry enough to be springing back into its normal uncontrollable curls. He didn't envy her the idea of trying to brush it out once it was all the way dry, and that thought just reminded him that he hadn't combed his own hair in at least a day. His mother would be so ashamed of him! His time in the Up-and-Under had been a long process of becoming more and more disheveled, and she'd probably turn away and say he wasn't her son at all if she could see him now.

The thought made his stomach feel all funny and unsettled, and so he pushed it away just as hard as he could, focusing on moving his hand down to Zib's shoulder. "Here," he said. "I'm right here."

"Avery!" She moved closer, until he had to bend his arm to keep from losing hold of her, and then she dropped abruptly away as she sat. He felt her hand grasp his ankle. "Where are we?"

"Still inside the mosasaur, I guess," he said glumly, and sat down beside her. She leaned, wrapping her arms around his shoulders in a brief but tight embrace before letting go and settling with her shoulder pressed to his, and the warmth of her skin just made him think about how cold he *wasn't*. The Saltwise Sea had been plenty cold, and when the improbable road had disappeared from underneath them, he'd been half-afraid he'd drown before he could swim, but here, it was warm and pleasant, even if they were still soaking wet. "It swallowed us, and it'll probably digest us down soon."

"I will do no such thing," said a deeply affronted voice, rich and warm and seeming to echo from absolutely everything around them. "Are you children *entirely* uncivilized? I am only here because my Lady of Salt and Sorrow asked that I should be, and while Seiche does not command the great beasts of the deep, we all love her well enough to listen when she calls for us, but I can go on my way easy as anything, and leave you to your previous destination."

There was a warning note in the voice that made Zib think she wouldn't have enjoyed whatever destination the mosasaur—because it simply *had* to be the mosasaur, they were inside the mosasaur, and the voice sounded like the one she heard in her head when she tried to talk without letting her teeth unclamp or moving her jaw—was talking about.

"No," she said hurriedly, before Avery could say anything. She adored him so, but sometimes his dedication to the logical way of doing things could result in his saying things that caused more problems than they solved. "We're very civilized. Why, we go to school and can do our sums and read books and everything!"

"Is that what you think it means to be civilized?" The mosasaur sounded genuinely curious. "That you could eat thinking people like sardines, but it would be all right, because you can do your *sums*?"

"Avery didn't mean it," said Zib. "It's just he's never seen a mosasaur before, and we didn't precisely have time for introductions before you were swallowing us, and it's only natural he should be a little bit confused." A dreadful thought occurred to her. "We weren't alone in the water. We had two friends with us: a drowned girl, Niamh, and the Crow Girl, who doesn't have a name, because crows don't have names the way people do. Do you know where they are?"

"In my stomach," said the mosasaur.

"Aren't we in your stomach?" asked Avery.

"No," said the mosasaur. "I had to keep swallowing after I swallowed you, or they would still be up in my mouth where they might get chewed by mistake, and the water I swallowed with them washed you out of my stomach and into my intestine. If you follow the wall back up, you should come to the chamber where they are. They're awake now, and moving around, but your Crow Girl became birds when she saw me coming, and I don't think she can figure out how to find herself and become a person again without help. So it will be a while before they come looking for you."

"What if we followed the wall down instead of up?" asked Zib, who was endlessly curious and always wanted to understand her options when she possibly could.

"You would come to the end of my intestines and have to pass through my cloaca, which would be unpleasant for you and painful for me, and end with you floating in the middle of the Saltwise Sea, where I would *not* swallow you a second time," said the mosasaur, almost primly. "I would recommend against it."

"Where are you taking us?" asked Avery.

"The Lady said you were following the improbable road back to dry land," said the mosasaur. "Big dry land, not a little island or atoll, which would be so much easier. How do you feel about conconuts?"

"Do you mean coconuts?" asked Avery. "They're very hard to open. I don't think I like them very much."

"No," said the mosasaur. "Conconuts are something else altogether, but if you don't know what they are, I suppose you wouldn't want to spend the rest of your life eating them, and I'll have to do what the Lady asked of me." It sighed, heavy as a shroud, the sound reverberating through every surface around the children like the banging of a gong. "I am taking you to the shore of the big dry land. It should take us most of the day. If you go back to the stomach, your friends are there, and you can find some of the fish I swallowed along with you and make yourselves a meal. I won't be able to talk to you while you're there, but you'll be safe there, and I promise not to swallow anything that's going to hurt you before I get you where you need to go."

The idea of eating raw fish made Avery's own stomach turn over, although he was sure that eventually he'd be hungry enough for it to start seeming like a good idea, even if it didn't seem like a good idea now. Asking if they could start a fire inside the mosasaur seemed like an even worse idea than eating the raw fish would be.

Zib, though . . . Zib stood, grabbing his hand and pulling him along with her, before asking politely, "Won't we be stealing your dinner if we sit in your stomach not being food and eat all of your fish?"

"It's not stealing if I say you can have it, so don't worry about that," said the mosasaur. "And I can eat so much fish in a day that taking as much as feeds four children—or three children and a flock of crows—isn't going to hurt me any. You can have as much as you like. Sometimes I pass atolls where there are conconuts floating in the water. If that happens today, I'll swallow those, too, so that you can find out what you've been missing!"

Avery squeezed Zib's hand harder and said,

"Thank you," to the air before he turned his face toward her and asked, more quietly, "Do you know which way is up and which way is down?"

"The water is moving past our feet in one direction and not the other," said Zib. "I think that's down, since water usually runs downhill."

Avery wasn't as sure about that as he would have been before the Up-and-Under, but still he nodded and said, "Then we go the other way."

"The other way."

They began walking, hand in hand, through the darkness, deeper into the body of the monster that had either rescued or consumed them, and neither of them was willing to even consider letting the other go.

FOUR

THE MEASURE OF A MURDER

"How many crows *are* you?" asked Niamh crossly, with crows sitting on every inch of her arms, head, and shoulders, their sharp little talons pricking at her skin. Every time she felt like she'd collected the last one, she would hear more cawing or rustling feathers from another direction, and have to feel her way through the dark until she found the missing bird.

Not all of them had been found alive. She'd stumbled over three different drowned birds, sad little piles of feathers on the floor, not moving, not breathing. In all three cases, the darkness had allowed her to conceal what she'd found from the rest of the murder, standing up straight and asking brightly if there were any more crows in the range of her voice.

How much space could there possibly *be* on the inside of a sea serpent? She'd seen them before, from a distance, but had never been inside of one. She only knew that sometimes the Lady of Salt and Sorrow would send them to save her children when they wandered into dangerous seas. No matter how far she walked, she never seemed to bump into a wall, and there was always another crow to find. Surely she had to be most of the way to a murder by this point. She had seven for a secret clustered on her shoulders alone.

Another crow croaked from the dark ahead of her, and somehow, that was the last straw. Niamh stopped where she was and sat down on the warm, slick floor, folding her arms. The action dislodged almost a dozen crows, and they cawed angrily.

"I told you," she said, tone sullen. "I told you I wasn't going to keep carrying you just because you wanted to be birds for as long as you could. I told you I was only going to help until enough of you was in one place for you to come together again. I *told* you, and I don't think you listened nearly as well as I needed you to. Maybe that's my own fault. Maybe I shouldn't expect good listening from birds. I don't know. I just can't keep doing this. I'm done."

The crows began hopping off of her, one by one, their feathers a rustle in the darkness. The last crow hopped down, and as she sighed and sagged, too tired to go any farther, there was another sound, soft and strange and almost impossible to hear, even in the quiet of the cavernous room around them.

Then, in a very soft voice, the Crow Girl said, "I'm sorry."

Niamh didn't reply.

"I didn't *mean* to not do what you said to do, it's just . . . now that I'm all one thing again, I know you told a piece of me that you were only going to carry me—us—me long enough to bring as many pieces as you could back together. And all of us appreciate it! But one crow isn't a lot of space for big thoughts. Crows are smarter than people think they are. That doesn't mean they're all the way as clever as how girls can be. So you told one piece of me, and that piece knew we were supposed to go back to being a girl as soon as we possibly could, but the rest of me didn't know. I'm sorry."

Niamh sighed. "I'm tired."

"I know." There was another rustle of feathers as the Crow Girl sat down beside her in the dark. Niamh leaned over, intending to rest her head against her friend, and almost fell to the ground as she found no shoulder where she expected one to be. Catching herself against the floor, she asked, "Where *are* you?"

"I'm here," said the Crow Girl. "I'm just . . . not finished."

Niamh didn't know quite what that meant. She

sat up straight again, trying to figure out how to ask what she wanted to know, and was still trying to figure it out when she heard someone who wasn't her or the Crow Girl moving in the dark. "Hello?" she called. "Is someone there?"

"Niamh!"

Niamh began to laugh to herself, quietly. She had never once been so happy to hear Zib's voice. Although . . . "Is Avery with you?"

"I'm right here," said Avery, with a little more restraint, a little more weariness, than Zib's effervescent delight. "Is the Crow Girl with you?"

"You could ask me yourself, you know," said the Crow Girl. "I have enough of me for asking."

"Fine," said Avery. "Are you with Niamh?"

The Crow Girl's laughter joined Niamh's. "I am—or some of me is, at the least—and now there you are, and now here we are, all of us, together again, on the inside of something we can't see or understand."

"It's a mosasaur," said Zib.

"Prehistoric marine reptile," said Avery, by way of explanation.

"So everyone's here," said Niamh, sounding utterly relieved. "I'm glad of it. I was worried you'd been swept away and lost, or . . ." *Or eaten.* ". . . something worse. But now you're here, and we can turn the lights on."

"I don't think there are any lights inside of a

mosasaur," said Zib, somewhat dubiously. She had read her big book of prehistoric creatures cover to cover several times, looking for new things to pretend to be afraid of when she was playing at being queen of the jungle, and she had never seen anything that would indicate the presence of lighting systems inside any one of them.

"Did you lose the sword when the mosasaur swallowed you?" asked Niamh.

Zib felt for her waist. The sword she had been given all the way back at the river that ran between the realm of the King of Cups and the King of Coins was still strapped at her hip, hanging safely in its sheath. "No," she said.

"Have you tried drawing it?"

"I wasn't going to cut my way out of the mosasaur," said Zib, sounding horrified. "It's alive and it's been polite so far and we'd be underwater if I did that—however deep down it is right now—so we'd probably all drown except for maybe you and mosasaurs went all extinct a long, *long* time ago, so maybe this is the last mosasaur, and we'd be no better than poachers if we killed it, even if we killed it after it had eaten us all up."

"I didn't ask if you'd tried to *cut* anything, I asked if you'd drawn the sword at all."

"Oh," said Zib. "No, I haven't tried drawing the sword yet."

"I don't think you've ever had that sword in a

completely dark room before," said Niamh. She sounded like she was struggling with frustration, like she wanted nothing more than to start yelling about how she needed people to move more quickly, listen more closely, and do what she told them to. "Try pulling it out of its sheath, and see what happens."

"All right," said Zib. There was a silent pause, and then, bright as a lantern in a coal mine, a solid blade of light burst into existence. It glowed the lambent silver-white of moonlight, casting illumination over a wide-eyed, wondering Zib and a bewildered, de-lighted Avery, filling the previously pitch-black cavern with shifting, shivering shadows.

Niamh looked to her side, to the Crow Girl—and screamed.

Zib followed the progress of her eyes, saw what Niamh had seen, and screamed in turn, dropping the sword. They were all of them very fortunate that it landed flat on the surface of the mosasaur's stomach, not tip-down and jagged as a broken bone, but none of them would know that for quite some time, as the glow had winked out like an extinguished candle as soon as Zib let go. The darkness came surging back, seeming all the more absolute now that they had had a glimpse of the light. It was almost welcome after what they had seen.

Strangely, it was Avery—calm, practical Avery—who recovered his wits first. "Crow Girl?" he said. "Are you—are you all right?"

"I'm enough to speak and reason," she said, sensibly enough. "I'm not as much more than that as I would like to be, the world being perfect and everything being as I'd like for it to be. If you can put the light back on, you can find the rest of me, or whether there *is* a rest of me. Some of me drowned when we were swallowed, you see." She paused then, taking a moment to mourn the crows who were never going to be a part of her again. "They died and they're going to stay dead, because that's what dying means. But I'm not going to find new crows down here inside a whatever-you-said, so please put the light back on."

"All right," said Zib, and stooped down, feeling around until her fingers brushed the sword. Here, too, it was good that it had fallen flat; she only touched the side of the blade, and not either of the edges. Running her hand down, she found the pommel and picked the sword up, all without cutting herself once.

As soon as her hand closed around the hilt, the sword lit up again, cool moonlight filling the mosasaur's stomach.

It was a massive room, unnervingly red, walls smooth but not as even as they had felt, concealing a myriad of crooks and crannies. From every possible surface, the bright blue eyes of crows watched them, glinting in the reflected light. They ruffled their feathers and cawed, short and sharp.

More crows littered the ground, these ones unmoving, eyes dull. There were more living crows than dead ones, but Zib still counted at least a dozen before she stopped looking and turned her attention back to the unnerving sight of the Crow Girl, sitting next to Niamh on the smooth red ground.

Half of her was there, one leg, one arm, the left side of her throat, and almost all of her head, save for one eye and one ear. The rest of her was missing. The space where she seemed to have been cut away was covered in tiny gray feathers, like goose down—or crow down, more properly. Looking at it made Zib's skin crawl. She had never pretended the Crow Girl was human. It was hard to pretend that sort of thing about a girl who regularly turned herself into an entire flock of birds. But she'd never seen such a clear and undeniable piece of proof that whatever the Crow Girl *was*, she wasn't an ordinary person, not even a little bit, not even when she made herself look like one.

The Crow Girl looked at her and smiled. "Thanks for the light," she said, and broke into birds, no more than twoscore of them swirling in the place where half a girl had been. All of them began to caw, setting up a horrible ruckus, and from all around the cavern, more crows came, finally able to see well enough to find each other and to fly. They came together in a swirling black storm of feathers and yelling. Niamh scrambled to her feet, moving away. Avery and Zib took a step back.

The crows reformed into the Crow Girl, now with almost all of the pieces a girl would normally be expected to have. Only almost—her right arm was missing from the elbow down, and dark feathers sprouted at the joint where her elbow should have been. She looked at it and frowned.

"I guess I lost more birds than I thought I had," she said. Then she shrugged. "Oh, well. Either we'll wind up someplace that has crows and I'll be able to convince some of the local birds to join me, or the next time there's a nesting season, I'll break up long enough to court and carouse and make myself a few nests. It'll be fine."

"But you're missing a hand," said Avery, sounding awed and horrified in equal measure.

The Crow Girl looked at him and smiled, eyes twinkling with mischief. "I've been missing worse, in my day. Can't be a hive thing and not know that sometimes you might lose pieces of yourself. This is the most I've ever lost at once, though. I'll have to be very careful until I've got my numbers back up again. I'm not sure how much more I could give up before I became a different person, and they might not be your friend, the way I've been. Or they might be someone who went running to the Queen of Swords to say to her 'Sorry, sorry, I have always been your monster, I'm sorry, take me back again.'"

Her smile collapsed then, replaced by a look of

wounded dismay, like she couldn't believe that even an imaginary version of herself would be foolish enough to go crawling back to the Queen who had made her, who she had fled from before she met the rest of them. Then she shivered, smile surging back.

"But that doesn't need to happen, since all I've lost's a hand, and hands are easy! Two or three new crows to the murder and I'll be fit as a fiddle once again, you'll see for sure."

"All right," said Avery dubiously. He didn't know the rules that governed Crow Girls, not even after spending so much time with one, and he didn't want to argue.

"Our problem right now isn't the Crow Girl's hand, it's how we're going to get out of this moss-asaur that Zib says we're inside," said Niamh.

"*Mos*asaur," said Zib. "It came up from beneath us in the ocean, and you're a Drowned Girl. How do you not know what it is?"

"Back where you came from, you lived on the land, right? On the ground, probably in a house?"

"With my parents," said Zib, sounding subdued.

"And there were animals there? Animals and plants and birds and stuff?"

"Well, yes."

"Did you know them all?"

Zib blinked. "No. Not exactly. But I knew a cat from a cow."

"Would you know a cow from a camel and a camel from a capybara? Or would you just know you were looking at something you didn't recognize?" Niamh shrugged. "It was big, it came up out of the water, it looked like the sea serpents the Lady sometimes uses to run errands for her, and it swallowed us without chewing, so I'm guessing it's at least partways friendly, but I don't know for sure."

"We're in the stomach right now," said Avery. "The mosasaur can't talk to us here, but it can when we're down in the intestine. It said the Lady had sent it to get us back to dry land, and talked about something called a 'conconut,' which isn't the same thing as a coconut?"

"Not at all," said Niamh. "A conconut tastes like peppermint ice cream and hot chocolate at the same time, and they're one of the nicest things in the whole world."

"Well, the mosasaur is going to swallow some of them if they're in the water," said Avery. "And some fish for us to eat. We have permission to eat any fish we find down here, even if we can't cook it."

"Just have Zib cut it up with the sword, that will cook it," said Niamh.

Avery raised his eyebrows. "It seems like a very useful sword," he said. "Where did you find it?"

"And why did you give it to us?" added Zib.

Niamh looked between them, then shrugged.

"This seems like as good a time as any for a story," she said. "Sit down, and I'll explain."

Zib and Avery exchanged a look.

They sat.

Niamh began.

FIVE

THE STORY OF THE SWORD

"By now you know the Up-and-Under is in the service of the elements, and each of them belongs to a monarch," Niamh began. "The King of Cups owns the waters, for example, and the Page of Frozen Waters serves him, and the Lady of Salt and Sorrow was by his side. She may yet be again, if she decides to take him back, if the Page allows it. Not every monarch has a consort. The ones who do tend to last longer."

"We know all this," said Avery crossly.

"Why should the Page have a say?" asked Zib. "She serves the King, doesn't she?"

"Yes, but she's never left his side, and the Lady

has. If the Page objected loudly enough, the King might refuse to bring his consort home again."

"That doesn't make any sense," said Avery.

Niamh fixed him with a look. "There's no point to arguing with how much sense the truth does or doesn't make when we're all inside the same mosasaur—I like that word, it's much kinder than most of the things people from the land call the denizens of the deep depths, and it has a friendly sound to it. We'll get where we're going when we get there. If you want to hear the story of the sword, why I found it and why Zib has it, you'll be patient and let me tell it in my own way, and not whatever way you want me to."

Avery opened his mouth to say something else, and stopped as Zib slapped her hand over it, cutting him off before he could begin. "He won't interrupt anymore," she said. "I promise, even if he doesn't. I want to know. Please, tell me."

Niamh nodded, seemingly appeased. "All right. The consorts of the kings and queens are not kings or queens in their own right, because there can only be one crown to a quarter, and if they were to be crowned, we would have eight crowns, and that would be too many. But the Queen of Wands, who stands for fire and change and the bright burning lands of the Coalcatch Caverns, has never taken a consort, nor set one aside; she has only and ever ruled alone, singular and complete unto herself. And when she first took her place, the Lord of the previous queen was still in his place, and very angry to see a succession when he, himself, had never been in consideration for the crown."

Avery, who found this whole system of elemental monarchs very confusing indeed—a confusion that wasn't helped in any way by Niamh's somewhat convoluted way of delivering information, which seemed to sometimes twist back onto itself and tie the narrative into a bright knot before moving forward—frowned, and said nothing. Zib, who was less confused, was also less constrained.

"Why wasn't he in consideration?" she asked.

"The Lord of Ash and Anger was a fire-tied man, yes, absolutely, but when the previous Queen of Wands had taken him for a partner, he had been burning in the Kingdom of Coins, pledged to earth, and was only ever an ember. By allowing himself to become her consort, barely better than a Page, he had removed himself from any future consideration. Once a thing is changed into something new, it can't always be changed back, no matter how much it might want to be. You'll never be the people you were before you entered the Forest of Borders, not ever again."

"That isn't fair!" burst Avery. "We didn't know what we were doing!"

"For the Crow Girl, becoming a murder is as natural as staying a single creature," said Niamh.

"She didn't know when she broke into birds that she was about to be swallowed by a mosasaur, or that some of her would drown before they could get out of the water. Does ignorance bring back the birds she lost? Does telling the world she didn't know put the missing pieces of her back into place? Or are they gone, whether she knew or not? I drowned before I was old enough to have a hope of swimming. I didn't know what water *was*, much less that I couldn't breathe in it, and now I can, because I'm something other than I was. I didn't know what I was doing. Does that start my heart beating again, and turn my skin warm and dry and wring the water from my hair? Or do I remain a subject of the Lady of Salt and Sorrow because I dove too deep when I didn't understand the consequences?"

Avery said nothing, but crossed his arms and looked sullenly at the wall. Niamh nodded in satisfaction.

"Knowing or not knowing makes no difference; some changes are for always, and when the Lord of Ash and Anger allowed the last Queen of Wands to lay her mantle over his shoulders, he became her creature. Some say she chose him because she recognized the hunger in his eyes, the need to burn and burn and burn forever, and so she made him over in her own image before he could set fire to the things she loved. Some say that's a charitable way of looking at a queen who never once in her reign did anything for the good of anyone else."

"Which is true?" asked Zib.

"Oh, how should I know? I'm a Drowned Girl. The mechanics of the forge have never been my concern." Niamh shrugged. The Crow Girl frowned at her.

"She did it because she wanted to save the Princess of Sparks," she continued. "She could see that the girl would be the next to wear her crown, when the time was right, and more, that he would destroy her if he was given half the chance. So she took him out of consideration in the only way she knew, and made him her almost-equal to fill his stomach with embers and his veins with fire and never regretted what she'd done where anyone could see."

"Oh," said Zib, voice small.

"So they lived together, the Queen, the Lord, and the Princess, and it was not until he began to realize he'd been tricked that anything went wrong again. He had thought, somehow, that he would be different; that he, for the first time out of anyone, ever, would go from Lord to King, and be able to sideways-walk his way into a crown. And when he realized that would never happen, he went to the royal forge, and he told them the Queen wanted him to have a weapon of his very own," said Niamh. "It was not so unbelievable, after all; a Lord or a Lady is very similar in position to a Page, and Pages will almost always have a weapon with which to defend their regent. So he asked for a sword, and the royal smiths set out to make him the finest sword they could, because it would be a representation of their lady when he carried it out into the world."

Zib looked at the glowing blade in her hand with new respect. "Is this the sword?" she asked.

Niamh nodded. "They carved a slice out of the sky above the Coalcatch Caverns, and they heated and hammered it into a blade sharp enough to slice through smoke. Which meant it had to be sharp enough to cut the wind as well, and that, along with its nature, put it halfway into the keeping of the Queen of Swords. All swords belong to her, much as all monsters do, and she swings them as she sees fit."

"Oh," said Zib. She looked at the sword again, now with discomfort. It was plain that the idea of holding something that belonged to the Queen of Swords made her uncomfortable, but her fingers remained closed around the hilt, keeping the blade lit. "Can she . . . does she see through the swords?"

"No. They aren't her eyes," said Niamh. "They're just a part of her domain, that's all. But this sword was made in the Kingdom of Wands, from sky and spark and smolder. There's sunlight in the making of it, and so it lights up when it's held by someone with enough fire about them to remind it of where it came from. That's you, Zib. You'd belong to the Kingdom of Wands if you stayed here, and didn't follow the improbable road all the way home again."

"But how did you get the sword?" asked Zib.

"Well, when the previous Queen of Wands looked to the Princess of Sparks and saw that she was almost ready to ascend, and saw her own fires growing low, and she was growing tired, she realized that if she wanted the girl she had raised for her own to have an easy ascension, she would need to clear the field of challenge as much as she possibly could. Naming the Lord to his title had removed him from consideration, but not from the possibility of challenge. He could never be King. He could still have presented a barrier to the young Princess, if he had decided it was in his best interests to do so—and by that time, she had been with the man for long enough to know that he would always think keeping someone else from power was in his best interests, for power in another's hands was power not in his own. So her final act of rulership was to challenge him for every slight he had ever committed against her, every insult he had ever offered, and she met him atop the mountains that shelter the Coalcatch Caverns, under the shadow of the Smokesmirched Sky, and she unleashed every power that was hers to command against him.

"I wasn't there for that fight, being safe at home in the city of my mother, frozen deep beneath the surface of the water, still years from the thaw and exile that waited for me, but its echoes rippled through the land for many reasons. The sky caught flame from one end of the Up-and-Under to the other, and while we don't keep proper calendars in the city at the bottom of the world, it's possible that the heat of that fight hurried our hundred-year thaw along, and I was able to surface years before I should have been. I don't know. I don't *want* to know, because knowing could only extend my exile from my home and people. She fought him for her people and her princess and her power, which had never been his to hold, and when it seemed he might defeat her, she called upon the old alliance between Swords and Wands to fan her flames with a westward wind. She blazed bright as any inferno for all the time it took to strike him down, and his blade fell into the river rushing by, into the land of the King of Cups, becoming one of the lost treasures that litter its bed. So when there was need for a way to stand against him, back in his land, I went to the bottom, and I grabbed the first weapon my hands could find, and I gave it to you, Avery, because Zib was a captive and I knew you would carry it to her. And now that she has it, it will burn for her, and never be extinguished again, because she is a creature of fire, and it knows her heart for tinder."

"What happened to the Queen?" asked Zib.

"What happens to a candle when someone blows

on it without ceasing?" asked Niamh. "She winked out, and the Princess of Sparks took her crown out of the ashes, and became the new Queen of Wands, and when the Impossible City called for fire ascendant, she went to take her place as ruler of us all, and she has held it ever since. When her time is done, she'll return to the Coalcatch Caverns and wait for fire to present her with a successor, and then she'll blow out like her predecessor did. Being Queen burns up everything they have, you see. It's not a job that leaves anything for after."

"I always thought that was sad," said the Crow Girl. "That they take children and raise them up as princes and princesses, not asking what they want, and then one day it's a crown and a choice they don't fully understand, and once it's made, they can't go anywhere else or do anything else or be anything else, not ever. Not unless they find a way to set their crown aside."

"The way you set aside your name?" asked Avery.

"I don't guess a queen or a king could go to another queen and ask to be turned into a murder of crows," said the Crow Girl. "If they could, we'd be running out of monarchs all the time."

Zib opened her mouth to say something, and was cut off as a wave of water came rushing down the dark tunnel of the mosasaur's throat, washing over them almost as high as their waists. She squeaked, shrill

and startled. The Crow Girl clutched Niamh, terrified, but did not break into birds, not this time—she
had learned her lesson. The water rushed by, leaving
the four children and the glowing sword unmoved,
and when it passed, it left several things behind.

Fish, flopping out the last of their lives in the sudden absence of the watery world that had always
been their home and haven. The irregular green
lumps of fresh coconuts, with their hulls still intact,
and the hairy brown spheres of coconuts that had
already been stripped of that outer layer of protection. And lastly, a sort of long, lumpy oblong with a
leathery-looking skin in shades of blue and purple.

Niamh clapped her hands in evident delight.
"Conconuts!" she said, gleefully. "Go on, Zib, cut
one open! I'm starving!"

When she spoke, Zib's stomach rumbled, and she
realized she was hungry too—if not hungry enough,
quite yet, to try eating fishes she had been forced to
gut for herself. She leaned over and grabbed one of
the lumpy fruits. It was surprisingly heavy, dense as
a melon, and almost the length of her forearm.

Gingerly, she placed it against the edge of her
blade and pushed. The sword cut through the fruit
with effortless ease, and the smell of chocolate and
peppermint—exactly as promised—filled the air
with sweetness.

Inside the fruit, the exposed flesh was a pearly

white, dotted with tiny black seeds, like specks of pepper. Niamh snatched half the conconut out of Zib's hands and leaned back, offering it to the Crow Girl. Zib took this as a suggestion, and held the other half out toward Avery.

"Here," she said. "I can't put the sword down without turning the lights out, so you should get yours first, and then I'll let the light go off long enough for me to eat."

Avery hesitated. She smiled.

"It's okay, really. I can wait a minute."

Meanwhile, the Crow Girl was shaking her head and pushing the fruit Niamh offered her away. "No, thank you," she said. "I'll just eat fish." And she turned hungry eyes on one of the still-flopping fish that littered the floor around them.

"They're raw," said Niamh, in case the Crow Girl hadn't noticed.

The Crow Girl smiled. "I'm a flock of scavengers," she said, and broke back into birds, launching themselves into the air and swarming around the nearest gasping shape. They began to peck and tear at it while half the murder was still landing, and while the fish died quickly, it kept moving for quite some time, pulled back and forth by the jerking of their beaks.

The murder didn't eat quietly. They cawed and flapped and poked at each other as they ripped the fish to pieces. Zib, as the only one without food of her own, grimaced and looked faintly horrified, but turned her attention back to the sword she was holding resolutely in front of her.

Avery took a cautious bite of the conconut, chewing and swallowing before his face transformed into a look of purest delight. "Why, this may be even nicer than the flavor fruits!" he said. "It tastes like summer! Zib, you have to try this!"

"Run it against the sword to cut it in half," she said.

He looked reluctant, as if even the idea of giving up this glorious treat was upsetting to him, but pressed the fruit against the sword, so that his half fell into two more halves, and each of them could eat a quarter. He swallowed before passing Zib her portion, then glanced to the other conconuts on the floor, as if reassuring himself that there would be other chances.

Balancing sword and fruit wasn't the easiest thing Zib had ever done, but by giving each of them a hand, she was able to bring the conconut to her mouth, and followed Avery's trail into satisfaction. Sometimes trying new things can be difficult, even when one is not riding in the belly of a great prehistoric beast. Zib had never been the most adventurous of eaters, preferring familiar meals and comfortable recipes, but since coming to the Up-and-Under, almost everything she'd eaten had been new, and so much of it had been wonderful that she couldn't imagine how she was going to go back home and go back to not having those things anymore.

The conconut didn't have the shifting tastes of the flavor fruit or the specific sweetness of the bonberries, but it was delicious in a whole new way, and she couldn't imagine wanting to eat anything else. Maybe ever again. In very little time, the whole piece was gone, and she cast around until she found another, slicing it the same way she'd sliced the first and distributing the pieces among the three of them. The Crow Girl was still a flock of crows rather than a person, and she didn't want any fruit anyway. They ate, and were still eating when the Crow Girl came back together into a single person, looking suddenly nervous.

"We're going up," she said. "In the water, I'd guess, unless mosasaurs can fly, but we're going up, and we're going up really fast."

Zib blinked. It made sense that birds might be able to tell the difference between being very high and being very low, and so she didn't feel the need to question the Crow Girl, who sounded very sure, and more than a little bit afraid. "Well, what does that—" she began.

She didn't get to finish, as a fresh wave of freezing water suddenly rolled down the mosasaur's throat and washed them all, hard, to the back of the stomach. The Crow Girl screamed, a shrill, terrified, human sound. Zib coughed and sputtered, fighting to keep hold of the sword. The water abated, leaving them plastered against one of the fleshy walls.

"I have to sheathe this or I'm going to lose it," she said, a little desperately. Niamh, who was the only one of them not coughing from the water she'd inhaled, nodded.

"Do it," she said.

Zib shoved the sword back into its scabbard. The light winked out instantly, leaving them back in absolute darkness. Avery reached for her arm, grasping her wrist, and she wrapped her free hand around his elbow, inching closer to him. The two children clung to each other in the black, and they were still clinging to each other when another wave of water hit, harder than the first one, unrelenting, unending.

It just kept on coming, until there was no air left in the mosasaur's stomach, until they were all holding their breaths, unable to see, unable to scream, unable to do anything but huddle in the cold and feel the current shoving them along, out of the stomach into the intestine, and then on from there, unending, unceasing, until—with a final, terrible pressure, like being squeezed through a short rubber tube—there was a pop, and they were floating in open, shallow water.

It was warm, especially compared to the water inside the mosasaur, which was now a dark shape in the water ahead of them. It swam forward another ten or so feet before banking lazily and swimming back toward them. Viewed from the outside and without the immediate panicky possibility of drowning, it was even more terrifying, vast and slatey gray with a long jaw bristling with teeth.

But it had kind eyes. Zib tried to focus on that, even as she thrashed in the water to reach for the surface, glad that she had her sword bolted securely at her hip, where it wouldn't be lost.

The mosasaur reached her and slid beneath her in the water, smoothly slicing through the waves. It began to rise, and she found herself sitting astride its long neck as it surfaced. She gasped when her head broke the surface, greedily sucking in a great breath of sweet-tasting air. She thought there had never been another breath as good. Someone coughed behind her.

She twisted around, and there was Avery, sitting much as she was, coughing into his hand. The Crow Girl was behind him, not sitting, but sprawled across the line of the mosasaur's backbone like a sack of mail thrown over the withers of a horse, her feathery black hair sticking out in all directions, her eyes closed. That would have been worrisome, if she hadn't been panting, making it obvious that she was alive.

Niamh was nowhere to be seen. *That* would have been worrisome, if it had been anyone other than their resident drowned girl.

"Are you children all right up there?" asked the

mosasaur. Its voice was louder outside of its body, but softer at the same time, like it had been wrapped in insulating cotton and transformed into the voice of a favorite teacher, someone beloved and capable of infinite affection. "I'm sorry I had to expel you like that, but there was no other good way, aside from making myself sick, and you'd have liked being vomited up even less."

The very thought made Zib feel queasy. "Yes, thank you, that would have been awful," she said. She didn't want to think very hard about how they *had* been expelled from the mosasaur, but the idea of being thrown up through all those teeth was a terrible one. She paused, two thoughts occurring to her at the same time. "But if we came out your cloaca—you said that would be painful to you. Did we hurt you?"

"No," said the mosasaur. "I hurt myself helping you, which is quite a different thing altogether. If anyone is to be blamed, it's our Lady of Salt and Sorrow, who knew when she asked me to help you that I would have to swallow you like seeds to save you from the sea, because I had no other way of doing what she asked of me, and that once you had been swallowed, one of us would be hurt in getting you out again, either you in one direction or me in the other. I chose the better of the two options. Thank you for your concern, but I'm fine."

"Oh, good," said Zib, and voiced her second thought. "You *are* a mosasaur, aren't you?"

"Why, yes," it replied, sounding charmed—although it was difficult to say whether it was more pleased to have been recognized or by the order of her questions, which showed more concern for its wellbeing than for her own accuracy. "I am, as were my parents before me, as will be my pups who are yet to come. There have always been mosasaurs in the Saltwise Sea."

"There aren't any mosasaurs where we come from, not anymore," said Zib.

"Then I am doubly glad to have met you, for everyone deserves to meet a mosasaur sometime in their lives," said the mosasaur. "Your friends are very quiet. Are they well?"

Zib looked to Avery and the Crow Girl. Avery was searching the line of the horizon, a pleading expression in his eyes, like he wanted nothing more than for all of this to be over. The Crow Girl had rolled onto her back and was staring, wide-eyed, at the sky, chest heaving with the effort of her breath. There was still no sign of Niamh. There was also no sign of a shore.

"They look okay," she said. "Why did you surface now? Where are we?"

"Ah," said the mosasaur, with slow understanding. "You had a sword at your hip, and I thought that

61

meant you served the Queen, and as the improbable road had been carrying you in this direction, I simply finished what it began. I'm sorry. I thought you'd be able to see the cliffs from here."

And it began to move, slicing through the water as it swam toward another bit of endless blue. Then the air shimmered around them, like the surface of a soap bubble, dancing briefly with rainbows and heat distortions, even as it remained cool against their skins.

Transitions are always complicated things when they happen outside the Forest of Borders, and even inside the Forest, they carry complications of their own kind. Sometimes a place cannot be seen until one is inside it, and then, once that final step has been taken, it becomes impossible to believe that a thing could ever have been less than utterly apparent. The air shimmered, soap-bubble-thin and tissue-tearable, and then, with a feeling like going very quickly up a very high mountain, or taking off in an aeroplane, the air ripped around them, and they were less than twenty feet from a long, rocky stretch of shore.

This was no sandy holiday beach. No one was going to build a cute little cottage here, although someone had taken the time to erect a lighthouse, a tall, needle-shaped structure cutting high into the gray-tinted sky. It wasn't cloudy, exactly, but it seemed fogged over in a way that Zib had never seen before, like someone was burning a very large fire so far away that the smoke was no longer a distinct column, but had spread out to cover everything, as all-encompassing as ink dripped into water.

The Crow Girl gave an ecstatic squawk and burst into birds without so much as sitting up, all of them taking to the air in a great flurry of wings and feathers, rapidly becoming inkblot stains against that gray-streaked sky as they darted for dry land.

"There," said the mosasaur, sounding pleased. "This is why I came to the surface. The Lady asked me to see you to land, and she said an atoll or an island would not be good enough, and so we are come here, to the lands of the Air, where the Queen of Swords and her winds reside, and here is where I will leave you, as I am a creature of water and you are not, and you could not be happy where I must go."

Zib, who did not particularly want to go before the Queen of Swords again, bit her lip. "I don't understand," she said, plaintively. Black specks dotted the shore where the Crow Girl's pieces had landed and were pecking at the rocks, hunting through them for tiny treats to scavenge from the surf.

It must have been a very simple thing, to be a crow. Zib envied it upon occasion.

Avery, who had not met the Queen of Swords, had not seen how perfectly, perilously beautiful she was, like a storm front rolling in on a wave of electric air, not yet close enough to douse and drown a garden, frowned at her. "What is there to understand?" he asked. "That's land. We need to be on land. Let the mosasaur take us to land."

"I don't understand how the geography works," she said, stubbornly. "Aren't you the one who likes things to make sense? We met the Crow Girl in the kingdom of the Queen of Swords, on the border of the kingdom of the King of Coins, and that was on the other side of an ocean. So how can we be coming to her lands *now*?"

"Ah!" said the mosasaur, in sudden understanding. "I see now why you're not sure of things. A kingdom is a form of protectorate, and there are four of them arrayed around the Impossible City like spokes of a wheel, or pages of a calendar, which are two things they have on the land and not in the depths of the sea, but which sailors have spoken of when they thought them relevant. It's amazing, the things someone thinks are important when they're about to be eaten!"

The mosasaur laughed. Avery blanched, realizing how easy it would have been for the mosasaur to chew them up instead of swallowing them whole, turning them into a meal and not passengers. "Do you eat people very often?" he asked.

"That's beside the point," said the mosasaur. "Your friend was asking about geography, which happens to be a keen interest of mine, as it's not a thing I'm ever likely to have much experience with. Water is mutable, but it always belongs to water. Neither the King nor the Lady believe in transforming their subjects into new shapes simply to let us see the world in ways we weren't designed for. The King of Coins is the same way. Both Queens are more reasonable when it comes to helping us adapt."

Avery frowned. He wasn't sure the word "reasonable" could be applied to the Queen of Swords, who was very fond of making monsters—she had made the Bumble Bear, after all, and all of the Crow Girls, which she created out of ordinary people and then gave away like they were toys she could dispose of whenever she cared to, and not living, feeling individuals who might not want to be given as gifts. But she was definitely willing to transform people into new shapes when she thought it was appropriate, and he could see how it might have been frustrating to spend a whole life in the water, when so many things were happening on the land.

Then again, if he were a mosasaur, or something else that lived in the water and thought thoughts like a person did, he might have felt the same way about people who had to spend their whole lives on the land when there were so many wonderful things happening down in the water. It was always so easy to envy the things someone else had, and not understand how good the things you had were. Why, before climbing the wall that shouldn't have been there, he had taken his bed and his pillow and his mother's spaghetti with meatballs and his toothbrush and his fine, shiny shoes very much for granted, thinking they were things that he would always have to call his own. And now, until they found the Queen of Wands and brought her back to the Impossible City to sit upon her throne and do her proper job, he had none of them, and sometimes—times like now, when he was sitting on the back of a sea monster in sight of the shore, and wanted nothing more than to go there and be properly dried off—he felt like he would never have any of those things ever again.

"A kingdom is the same thing as a protectorate, which isn't the same thing as a land," said the mosasaur. "A kingdom is like a country. It's an idea. It's a line on a map, and it could be different tomorrow than it is today, if people decide they want a new map, or a prettier map, or something altogether different. Kingdoms and countries rise and fall. They have a lifespan, just like every other idea. Lands, though . . . lands just *are*. They don't care where you draw your lines. They don't care what you say they're supposed to look like. You think a land changes because someone has a map? Well, maybe that's how it works where you come from, but that's not how it works in the Up-and-Under."

"But shouldn't a Queen stay in her land, not run around managing a kingdom?" asked Zib.

"A kingdom needs a Queen—or a King—the way a country needs someone to make the big choices and set the laws. A land doesn't need any of those things, as long as the people agree to listen to the rules their monarch makes even at a distance. So here in the Land of Air, they answer to the Queen of Swords, because it suits them to do so, and when she isn't here, they are still the Land of Air, and these are still the shores of the Land of Air, and when she is gone, they will have another Queen, or perhaps a King, to ignore as it suits them. But for now, your friends are on the shore, and I have brought you as far as I can without doing myself some further harm, and you should go."

"Friends?" Avery turned to the shore once again. The scattered shape of the Crow Girl had been joined by the slight, singular shape of Niamh, too far away for them to see the details of her face, but close enough to recognize. He waved. Niamh waved back.

"How do we get there?" asked Zib, sounding only somewhat mollified by the thought that perhaps the Queen of Swords wouldn't be in her own land at the moment.

"You swim, of course," said the mosasaur, and submerged, leaving the two children floating.

The water here was bitterly cold, even compared to the water they'd been doused with inside the mosasaur. Zib squeaked. Avery squawked. Both of them began swimming as hard as they could toward the shore.

Avery quickly fell behind, thrashing helplessly,

barely keeping his head above water. Zib circled back and put her arm around him, and together the two of them made for the shore.

The mosasaur had gotten them as close to land as possible, and with the waves at their back pushing them toward the shore, they were quickly in shallow waters, their feet brushing the earth even as their bodies remained buoyant enough to bob with every motion of the tide. Still they pushed forward, joined together, four legs kicking in the same direction, until they were able to stand upright and wade the rest of the way.

Niamh came running along the shore to join them—Avery wasn't sure he could call it a "beach," since there wasn't a grain of sand to be seen, just rocks on top of rocks on top of rocks. Small crabs that had yet to be caught by the Crow Girl scuttled between them, weaving in and out of clumps of kelp that seemed far less inclined to be helpful than the stuff they'd encountered on the other side of the well beyond the Impossible City, and fragments of shell stood out white as bone against the brown and gray. It was a bleak, unwelcoming landscape, and Avery shivered at more than the gust of wind that came cutting along the edge of the high cliff wall between them and the rest of the Land of Air.

"Air, they say," he muttered. "All I've seen so far is rocks and water."

"What?" asked Zib.

"Nothing," he said, more than halfway sullen. They walked, barefoot, up the rocky shore, and Avery was suddenly grateful to be so cold. The rocks couldn't hurt his feet if he couldn't feel himself stepping on them.

Niamh was there to meet them. "You look cold," she said.

"We are," said Avery. "We're still alive, remember? You're only not cold because you're drowned."

"True enough," she agreed. "But you need to get warm, and the Crow Girl needs to find some more crows to be a part of her, so we should head inland. Did you say goodbye to the mosasaur?"

"Not really," said Zib. "She didn't give us the chance."

"Oh. Well, the path up the cliff is this way." Niamh turned away, waving for the pair of them to follow.

Avery and Zib exchanged a look before they shrugged and did exactly that, letting her lead them across the rocky shore to where the pieces of the Crow Girl were pecking at the skittering crabs. Several of them looked up as the children approached, giving warning caws that turned into a cacophony as the whole murder rose into the air and swirled around the trio, wingtips brushing their cheeks.

Niamh laughed and kept on walking. Zib and Avery, and the pieces of the Crow Girl, followed.

There was no path along the shore, which was too rocky to have allowed it, and so they cut straight across to the cliff wall. Up close, it was more visibly something porous than it had been from a distance: sandstone, maybe, or limestone. Various small channels had been worn into it, twisting and looping back on themselves like playground slides. Not all of them came out at ground level. Some were set so high into the cliff that Avery couldn't imagine them being of any use to anyone who didn't have wings, and even they might have had trouble with the winds that high up.

Niamh led them to a channel that opened only about a foot above the ground, stepping up and turning to offer them her hands. Avery, whose feet had started to thaw and hurt a little from all the rocks underfoot, took the offered boost eagerly, letting her half-pull him onto the trail. Zib was only a step behind.

The stone of the cliff was a pale shade of pearly gold, and it was surprisingly warm to the touch. Avery blinked, looking down at his aching feet. "What is this stuff?" he asked.

"They call it skystone here," said Niamh. "It absorbs the sun when the smoke allows it to shine, and so they have warmth all the time. People quarry it to heat their homes and their nests. If you pick up even a pebble, you'll never be cold again."

"Really?" asked Avery. He looked at the path around his feet with new interest, but didn't see any pieces of the yellowish stone.

"Let's get to the top," said Niamh. She began walking, away from the Saltwise Sea and the stony shore, and the others followed, two on foot and one who was many soaring overhead, and no one remained to watch them go.

SIX

MAKING
ILL-CONSIDERED WISHES

The gentle warmth of the stone was enough to soothe some of the ache out of Zib and Avery's feet even as they finished thawing and kept walking onward without shoes between them and the world. Their time in the mosasaur had taken the edge off their hunger and rested their legs, and they were easily able to make the climb up the relatively shallow, sloping hill. The cliff was sheer, but the channel had clearly been cut for easy walking.

"Who made this?" asked Avery. "We don't know anything about the people who live here, or what they're like."

"The Page of Ceaseless Storms opens the natural

ways here in the Air," said Niamh. "He likes it when his little breezes can make it down to the water and grow big and strong along the tideline, and so he cuts them channels to flow along, lest they break themselves on the cliff."

Avery blinked. "I thought the Pages were always bad," he said.

"They are," said Niamh. "They're heartless creatures, each and every one of them, and the Page of Ceaseless Storms would see you both drowned and dead—not consigned to my city beneath the ice, but bones at the bottom of the sea—if he thought it suited his aims. He'd find no wickedness in that, no wrong. But even a heartless thing can be gentle in its own way. He loves the winds. He nurtures and cares for them. And if you think that sounds sweet, keep in mind that a wind well-nurtured and fed by a loving enough hand can grow up to be a great twister and strike you dead where you stand."

Avery nodded, very slowly, and for a time, said nothing more as they climbed higher and higher.

Zib's stomach grumbled. She rubbed it with one hand, frowning. "I wish we had some more conconuts," she said.

"Don't," said Niamh, sounding alarmed.

There was a rumbling from overhead. Niamh flung her arms over her head, ducking like she expected something to hit her from above. Zib blinked, watching this. Avery, having slightly more of a sense of self-preservation, mimicked Niamh, and the Crow Girl squawked alarm before scattering through the air away from them. She made it clear barely a moment before a gust of wind whipped by, playfully tugging on the endless tangles of Zib's hair, and dumped a dozen or so conconuts on the girl's head.

Fruit, however delicious, still hurts when it hits someone. Zib yelped and cowered away from the impact—not quickly enough to shield herself from the beginning of it, but in time to cover her head from the end. As quickly as it had begun, the wind whisked away, leaving conconuts scattered all over the ground.

Zib straightened, blinking. Niamh uncovered her own head, looked at Zib, and sighed.

"That was one," she said. "I'm sorry. It never occurred to me that I would need to say anything. The rules of Air are so well-known that I didn't think to explain them."

"Remember that there's *nothing* well-known about your world where we're concerned, and explain next time," said Zib, hotly. She wasn't angry at Niamh, exactly, but she didn't care for being showered in falling fruit, and her head was aching.

"You may as well gather it up," said Niamh. "It belongs to you, and you'll pay for it whether you eat it or not."

"Pay for it how?"

"In the Land of Air, words carry," said Niamh.

"If you make requests, or wishes, the winds can choose to bring you what you've asked for, but they always collect the cost eventually. Sometimes it's an act of malice. Sometimes it's merely an expectation of a favor granted."

"And sometimes the Lady of Salt and Sorrow, who you *knew* had been found, and didn't tell me about, sends a sea monster to carry her spies into my lady's lands, and so I don't see them as I should have done," said a voice from behind them. "Not until someone wishes on a cloud and the little zephyrs come racing to tell me that we have intruders in our midst, and I should come as quick as cumulus if I want to whisk them away into nothing."

The group turned in slow, unified horror, staring. Behind them on the path stood a small boy with gray skin and white hair, holding a trident carelessly in one hand and frowning at them. His clothes were wet. His skin was not.

"Well?" said the Page of Ceaseless Storms. "Do you deny that you came here as spies for the Lady?"

The three children and a handful of nearby crows continued to stare. The Page's frown grew into a scowl.

"When I ask you a question, you answer it," he said, and while his voice was young and piping, his tone was ancient and sepulchral. It was as if the spirit of a very ancient, somewhat terrible man had been pushed into the body of a very small boy, displacing whatever had been there to begin with—and as this land belonged to the Queen of Swords, who made monsters the way some people make daisy chains, it was possible that was exactly what had happened.

"We're not spies for anyone," said Avery. "Spies are wicked people who want to undermine the rightful government of the United States of America, and we wouldn't be spies if somebody tried to make us!"

The Page cocked his head. "What's a United State of America?" he asked. "Because it sounds like you just admitted to being agents of a foreign government, here in my lady's lands to undermine her."

"No, no," said Zib hurriedly. "The United States is the government in the world where we come from, which is very far away from here on the other side of the Forest of Borders, and we don't work for the government. They only hire grown-up people like our parents. We're just trying to find the Queen of Wands so we can take her back to the Impossible City and she can show us how to go home!"

It sounded so simple, when she laid it all out in a line like that. It sounded like the most impossible thing anyone had ever said in the history of words. The Page blinked. The Page looked, for an instant, utterly baffled. Then the Page smiled, suddenly sweet as the sunshine in the spring, warm and gentle and appealing.

Even springtime sun can burn. Avery tensed as the Page opened his mouth to speak.

"The Queen of Wands," said the boy, "is missing?"

The owls had said it was possible the other monarchs knew and were keeping that fact a secret so they could press their own plans for taking the throne, but that it was also possible the disappearance of the one queen who was meant to manage the entire Up-and-Under was still hidden from the lot of them, who had not tried to breach the bounds of the Impossible City since she vanished. Zib swallowed, mouth suddenly dry as she realized she had said something she shouldn't have.

Lying to the Page seemed like an even worse idea at this point than telling him the truth, and so Zib only nodded, committed to this choice.

"I see," said the Page, and turned, placing two fingers in his mouth. He whistled, sharp as anything, sharp and shrill and sustained, a high, rising note that should have exhausted his lungs and left him gasping for air. Instead, it went on and on without end, soaring into the sky, until it seemed like it must be a physical thing.

Zib clapped her hands over her ears and squeaked, the sad protest of a creature in pain, and still the Page ignored her and kept whistling. And then he stopped, and turned to smile beatifically at the group of them.

"There," he said, sounding pleased with himself. "That should do it. None of you move. You're my property now."

Zib, who felt responsible for the entire situation, looked down at the fruit still littering the ground. "Can we at least pick up the conconuts?" she asked, wistfully. "Only, I asked a cloud if I could have them, even if I didn't realize that was what I was doing when I did it, and that's why the little zephyrs told you we were here. It feels like we're being punished right now, and if we're going to be punished because of something I did, I ought to be able to finish all the way doing it before the punishing begins."

The Page nodded magnanimously. "I've never heard of a wish being wasted on an empty stomach before," he said, waving his free hand. "You only get three. Most people ask for something much bigger and better than a pile of fruit, no matter *how* hungry they are."

"I didn't know I got any wishes, much less three of them," protested Zib, and began gathering fruit from the ground all around them.

Meanwhile, Avery prodded Niamh with his elbow. "You know the rules we don't know yet," he hissed. "You know how many wishes we get, and what we can wish for. Can't you wish us out of this?"

"When I first came up from the city under the ice, I found myself on the rocky beach between the Land of Air and the Saltwise Sea," she said, regretfully. "I didn't know which way was right or open for me to go. I didn't know much of anything about life above the water, because why would I? That world was not, had never been, for me. I was too young when I drowned to have any attachment to air. Most people do, even Earth children like you, because you have to breathe. Even the mosasaur knew what it was to want for air. Drowned girls are anathema to the Queen of Swords, because we don't *need* her the way all the rest of you do, and she can't stand it at all. Makers of monsters want nothing more in all the world than they want to be needed."

The Page rolled his eyes but said nothing, allowing Niamh to say her piece.

"I went looking for a way home, and I stumbled over wishing without knowing what it was, the same way Zib did," she said. "I spent all three of my wishes before I caught any consequences in the net of my desires, and then the consequence I caught was the Page of Frozen Waters coming to carry me away to the King of Cups."

"I thought you said she took you while you were on the shore gathering stones," protested Avery, who was after all a very linear sort of child, and liked his stories to make sense, and didn't care one little bit for the shape of the story he was currently caught in. This was a Zib-shaped story, not an Avery-shaped story, and in an abstract sort of way, he felt that it was very unfair that they should be stranded together in something that only suited one of them.

"I went through my wishes very quickly," said Niamh, somewhat abashedly. "I wished a shinier stone, and then I wished I could stay on the shore longer, because I was having such a lovely time, and finally I wished I had someone to talk to."

"I heard that last one," said the Page, almost gleefully. "I called my cousin and told her she had a gift for her King in my lands if only she wanted to come and collect it, and that she'd be answering two wishes at the same time if she did. No one ever wishes for a Page, especially not her, and so she was very pleased to do as she was asked."

He looked so proud of himself that he didn't seem to notice the growing rage in Niamh's expression, until the dripping drowned girl launched herself at the Page, hands hooked into claws, scrabbling at him like she was going to scratch his skin away until he realized the depth of what he'd done.

"That was my *home*!" she shouted. "That was my whole *world*! I didn't realize what I was doing, I didn't understand, and you turned 'longer' into 'forever' and 'someone to talk to' into 'someone to take me prisoner and carry me away from everything I knew and everyone who loved me'! I'm trying to help *these* children go home because I can't!"

The Page recoiled, looking shocked and confused by her assault. Then he planted the butt of his trident in the center of her chest and pushed her away, slowly but seemingly without making any real effort, as if moving her were nothing to him, even though she was larger than he was by almost a foot. When he spoke again, his voice was as frozen as the city beneath the ice where Niamh belonged.

"What a wish costs is not left up to the one who does the wishing," he said. "It's not even left entirely up to the one who gives the answer. Not every cloud that carries a gift to a little girl comes running to tattle to me, or I'd be nothing more than a glorified delivery service for the petty wishes of the unprepared. When you ask the universe for a reward, you get what you get. I gave you everything you asked for, and I gave the King of Cups a gift in the same moment, and so I benefited my liege. I am a proper Page, and you would do well to remember your place, drowned girl. You have no right to judge me or the things I do. You have no right to be here."

"I'm only here because you trapped me," spat Niamh. "I won't let you trap these children."

"Oh, and what are you going to do to stop me?" he asked. "Drowned girl, water girl, so afraid of her own Page that she'll do anything to stay out of fresh water."

"I serve the Lady of Salt and Sorrow," she said, voice stiff. "I have no reason to listen to the Page of Frozen Waters, who serves the King but not the Lady. If the Knight of Wind and Waves wants to step to me, I'll answer their commands."

The Page rolled his eyes. "A Knight?" he asked. "May as well say you'd obey the Jack of whatever

damp thing you think deserves service. That's so ar-
chaic and old-fashioned! But what you want doesn't
matter. She owns you."

"People can't own people anymore," said Avery
sharply. "It's against the law."

"Maybe where you come from, and maybe where
you come from, the law actually has teeth," said the
Page. "Here, you can make all the laws you want,
and they won't change anything at all unless people
decide that they will. Most people won't decide for
something that makes their lives even the slightest
sliver of a sigh harder than it feels like it ought to
be. None of you belongs to me by nature, but that's
just because your hearts come in the wrong flavors.
If you were airy things, you'd have been mine from
the beginning. Which reminds me." He turned a
sharpened smile on the remaining crows, who had
been strangely silent through all of this, like they
were hoping they could slip by unnoticed.

"It's all right," he said. "You're an oddity, since my
lady gave you away to a better keeper, and we never
expected to see you here again. But you're so dwindled. It's not fair. Let me help you."

And he whistled for a second time, and the birds—
who must have been massing just on the other side
of the cliff since he sent out his first call, the rustle of
their feathers and the flapping of their wings muf-
fled by the wind through the canyon—came over the

stone barrier and swirled around the children. Zib squawked, barely keeping herself from dropping her dearly bought conconuts all over the ground.

Most of the birds were black-winged, some with gray heads, some without, but a few bright blue birds flew among the rest, their cries as raucous and their wings as wide. They swirled until they formed half a dozen figures, and then they were people, and not birds at all.

Five of them looked like they could have been the Crow Girl's sisters, wearing feather dresses that extended halfway down their thighs, lying flat against their skin, their hair almost exactly the same. Two of those were clearly Crow Girls, bright-eyed and sharp. One was smaller, slighter, and had bright blue feathered hair, matching her bright blue dress. The other two were larger, patchworked black and white, from their clothing to their hair.

The sixth figure was a boy, older than any of the others, tall and lanky, the sort of teenager Avery sometimes dreamt he might be able to grow up to become, if he ate his vegetables and did his chores and always, always listened to his parents. He had the vague idea that growing up to be one of the cool boys who swaggered through the high school fields with a book on their hip and a beautiful girl on their arm had something to do with being a very, very good child, as though social success and beauty were rewards for behaving well, like gifts from some sort of cosmic Santa Claus.

This new boy was dressed all in black, in a suit of feathers, and his hair was a steely gray that looked as feathery as the girls, only a few shades darker than his eyes. He cocked his head and looked at the lot of them, finally focusing on the Page of Ceaseless Storms.

"Children are not storms, no matter how confused you are on the issue," he said, almost patiently. "Why have you called us here?"

The girls were moving toward the still-scattered crows, cooing and cajoling. The crows, for their part, looked alarmed, but did not fly away; they held their ground, shifting from one foot to the other, digging their talons into the stone.

"*These* children came out of the Forest of Borders," said the Page. "They've been following the improbable road. *They* serve the Lady of Salt and Sorrow, and they told me the Queen of Wands is missing. These are all things our lady ought to know, don't you think?"

"They might be," said the boy, and turned his attention to the children instead. "Do you think you're relevant to our lady?" he asked, with utter politeness.

"Please, sir," said Zib. "We didn't mean to cause trouble or attract attention. We're not serving anyone—I mean, Niamh is from the city under the ice, so she serves the Lady of Salt and Sorrow, but not in any 'working for her' sort of way, more in a 'she's very cool and I like her a lot' sort of way—and we just want to follow the improbable road all the way to where we're meant to be."

"Do you?" The boy looked down at the ground, feathery eyebrows lifting. "But the improbable road isn't here right now."

"We sort of . . . lost it," said Avery.

"Lost it?" echoed the boy.

"We didn't mean to," said Zib, defensively.

"How does one lose a road?"

Zib blinked, then smiled, relieved to have found someone who seemed to know less than she did about the world they were crossing entirely on foot. "The improbable road was leading us across the surface of the Saltwise Sea, and I guess we upset it, so it popped, and now we don't know where it is, until we do something improbable enough that it shows up for us again. It's never where you think a road logically *ought* to be, meaning it's not here because this would be a very reasonable, logical place to put a road, or at least a footpath."

The boy frowned at her. "That seems a little bit more ridiculous than improbable," he said, after a moment's thought. "Shouldn't it be called the ridiculous road? At least then it would be alliterative. We like alliteration here in the Up-and-Under. It lends an air of symmetry to the things we can't undo, and that can be a very pleasant thing."

"I'm sorry, we haven't been introduced," said Avery, who was starting to feel as if they had entirely lost control of the situation. "My name is Avery Alexander Grey. It's a pleasure to meet you. And your name is . . . ?"

"I'm Jack Daw," said the boy. "I'm a jackdaw, the same way your friend is a Crow Girl, only not, because jackdaws are allowed to keep our names when we become a train, and Crows give theirs away for the sake of the murder."

Avery blinked, very slowly. "So . . . you're a jackdaw, and you got to keep your name, but your name is 'Jack Daw'?" he said.

"Yes, that's correct."

"But that doesn't make any sense at all!" Avery scowled. "Why did the Crow Girl have to give her name away if you get to keep yours? It isn't fair."

"It isn't, is it? But she knew what she was doing when she made her bargains, and I'm not the one to tell her she chose incorrectly. No one gets to tell her that, not anymore. Now, the Page tells us you're here in the service of the Lady of Salt and Sorrow. Is he correct?"

"I already told you no!" said Zib. "If you're asking Avery just because he's a boy, I'm going to—going to—!"

"Going to what?" asked Jack, with seemingly sincere curiosity. He looked at Zib. "Stomp your foot and yell? We're in the Land of Air, and you're a child of fire if you're anything. More, the Page says your Queen is missing. Who's to say that you're not here looking for mischief to make? I should whisk you off to the palace and let my mother deal with you."

"Your mother's not the boss of me," snapped Zib.

"My mother's not here right now, because she's off caring for her kingdom, but I assure you, she's the boss of everything in the Land of Air," said Jack. "My mother is the Queen of Swords, after all."

SEVEN
THE WINDWRACKED WILDS

Zib stared at him.

"She is not," she said, when the silence had grown too big and heavy to be allowed to hang between them any longer. "She can't be. She makes monsters, not boys!"

"And can't a boy be a monster?" he asked, and smiled at her. His teeth were straight and white and perfect. So perfect that they became somehow terrible. Teeth were a normal thing and not a nightmare because of their little imperfections, the chips, uneven edges, and discolorations. These were the teeth of a statue, and they looked strong enough to bite the throat out of the world.

"I can be a monster if I like," he continued, even as she shuddered and looked away. "I can spread my wings and carry tidings of doom across all the lands in the world, and they'll call me bad luck and ill omen and artificial boy, and it will all be worth it, because she learned so many things in the making of me, wonderful, horrible things—things she can use to make better monsters ever after. You wouldn't have your Crow Girl if not for me. Before she made me, Mother had never quite figured out how to make a thing of many hang together when she asked it to be one."

There was a squawk and a swirl and a wild flapping of wings as the crows finally stopped allowing themselves to be loomed over and leapt into the air, joining together in a swirling whirlwind of wings and feathers. The five girls who had come in with Jack Daw turned, almost as one, to look at him, and he nodded, very quickly. They jumped, and broke into birds, surging into the whirlwind, until everything was feathers and the sound of squawking.

Zib jumped when she felt a hand grab her elbow, almost dropping her armload of conconuts. The fruit seemed terribly important now, a whim that had caused them no end of chaos. She looked to the side, and there was Niamh, holding her tightly, pale, watery eyes filled with fear.

"Run," hissed Niamh, the word contained as much in the movement of her lips and the horror in her eyes as in the sound, which was all but stolen by the birds.

Zib nodded, and they ran, Avery at Niamh's other side as the three children fled from the cacophony, away from the strange boy who served the Queen of Swords, who might not mean them actively ill, but almost certainly meant them nothing good in the world. They ran and ran—swiftly at first, then with more effort as the slope of the hill began dragging them down, weighting their feet and slowing their steps. They ran until the high rock walls to either side of them fell away, and they were emerging onto a high mesa covered in short green grass and tiny white flowers, like puffs of perfumed cloud. A gentle wind caressed their skin, and nothing about the landscape offered any cover at all.

There was no place for them to hide. Still, they stopped, too tired from the run to go any farther. Zib finally dropped her armload of conconuts, sagging. "The Crow Girl," she said. "We left her behind. We have to go back and get her!"

"We can't," said Niamh. "She'll catch up with us, or she won't."

"What do you mean, she won't?" demanded Avery. "She always comes back."

"Crows can be surprisingly loyal that way," said Niamh. "But she's lost a lot of birds, and I don't know how many more she can give up and still come back together as anything even resembling herself."

"Not many," said a high, weary voice from behind them. The three turned as one and stared at what they found behind them.

A little girl stood at the mouth of the pathway down to the beach, younger than Avery or Zib, maybe five or six at best, small and soft and not quite finished in the way of very small children. When she spoke, it was obvious that several of her teeth were missing, and her eyes were too big for her face, enormous and very, very blue. Her hair was short, black, and spiky, clumping together like it was made of downy feathers, and her short black dress was equally feathery, dipping down to her mid-thighs before it stopped, abruptly. Her feet were bare, toenails a little overly long, like they were made for gripping.

"I lost too many," said the child, and walked unsteadily toward them, as if she wasn't quite sure of her balance. "I tried to come back together, and there wasn't enough of me to be a girl and stay alive. So I tried to remember who I was before I became the murder, and I realized it felt like I'd lost pieces of myself before, and always known they were missing, it just hadn't mattered enough for me to care about it. So I tried to think about coming back together to cover up those missing places, and then I was together, I was just smaller than I used to be." She smiled an uncertain, gap-toothed smile at Zib and Avery. "I don't think I can lose any more, though."

"Probably not," said Avery, in a strangled-sounding voice. Accustomed as he was becoming to the Up-and-Under's somewhat ridiculous brand of logic, the idea that a teenager could become a little kid again was unsettling to him. He didn't *want* to become a little kid. He also didn't want to do the wrong thing or make the wrong wish and wind up a teenager so old that his own parents wouldn't recognize him when he finally got to go home. "None of us knows how to take care of a baby."

"I've cared for drowned infants before, but never by myself, and I think living infants need different things than drowned ones do," said Niamh. "Yes. Better not to lose any more birds."

The Crow Girl stopped when she reached them, twisting the feathers at the bottom of her dress between her fingers and looking anxiously down at the ground. What must it have been like, to be standing on two legs and seeing the world from such a different perspective? Avery couldn't imagine it, not entirely. He knew his own view of the world had been lower down once, that he had been a child as small as she was, and before that, a toddler and even an infant, but what memories he had of that time were scant and hazy, half-dreamt things that could have happened to someone else altogether, and not really real to him at all. And the change from that perspective to the one that now felt natural and normal had come a little bit at a time, in the ordinary manner, so that it had never been jarring or even really noticeable.

"There's nothing to hide behind here," said Zib. "They're going to catch up to us. We need to keep running." She bent and began picking up conconuts off the mesa surface, gathering them meticulously into her arms. "How do we get down?"

"There's a path down the side, here," said Niamh.

Zib glanced up and frowned, looking at the drowned girl a little more closely. "You came from a city under the ice, and you weren't here very long before you say the Page of Frozen Waters carried you away and you wound up in that river in the King of Cups's kingdom," she said.

"Yes. That's right."

"So how do you know so much about the Land of Air? It doesn't seem like you had a lot of time for exploring."

"The Pages like to talk." Niamh shook her head, gesturing for them to follow as she moved closer to the edge of the mesa. They needed to keep moving, or they would surely be caught. "The Page of Frozen Waters maybe most of all, because she has no friends in her land, or in any others, except for the other Pages. So they would all come together from time to time, and they would talk about their lands, and their trials, and the things they wished their lives would become. The Page of Sleeping Riches hopes that one day his King will find someone he likes better and allow him permission to rest eternally in the deep halls of the earth, while the Page of Gentle Embers only wants more ways to burn. I know the way things work here because the Page of Ceaseless Storms knows everything his winds map out for him, and delights in the sharing of his secrets."

When she reached the mesa's edge, the stepped over it, and dropped out of sight. Avery and Zib exchanged a wide-eyed look before rushing after her, the Crow Girl staggering unsteadily behind.

The edge of the mesa was a sheer drop-off to a low and distant land far below them. A fall from this height would have been fatal to any one of them, and while they weren't completely certain Niamh *could* die—drowning being a form of dying, after all, and implying that she had already died at least once, and might not be able to do it again—they also didn't want to scrape her off the ground and carry her along with them in a jug or jar.

But there was no sign of her splashed across the ground below, which was something of a relief and something of a surprise.

"Look down," she said, reasonably enough.

Avery looked down.

A ridge ran around the edge of the mesa, like the second layer of a high-tiered wedding cake, wide and blanketed in soft green grass taller than the grass growing on the unsheltered top of the thing. It extended in both directions, and Avery could see that it was gently sloped, implying that it would be possible to follow it all the way down.

"Come on," urged Niamh. "We need to keep moving."

"I don't like falling," said Avery, and sat so that his legs were dangling over the edge, heels pressed to the rock. Gingerly, he inched himself forward, finally sliding off and landing a few feet below in the grass. He promptly fell down, landing on his bottom with a thump.

Giggling, Niamh offered him her hands and helped him up, then looked back to the watching Zib. "Your turn," she said.

"Catch my fruit," said Zib, and began dropping the conconuts down, one by one, for the others to retrieve. Avery tried not to be frustrated by how much time she was taking. She'd asked for fruit because she was hungry. They were almost always hungry in the Up-and-Under, where the meals were irregular if they came at all—and they didn't, always. Avery had grown up in a world where breakfast, lunch, and dinner happened at regular, predictable intervals, as dependable as the seconds on a clock. Now, food was a random and sometimes mysterious thing that happened when it happened and didn't when it didn't, and especially after her unconsidered wish had caused her so much trouble, he could understand not wanting to give up the only source of food they had.

And it wasn't like he could see anything else around here for them to eat. The wind was gentler on the ledge than it had been on the top of the mesa, and even there, it hadn't been strong enough to blow them away, but it blew unceasingly, and it didn't seem like the sort of thing that would encourage a lot of cooking, or agriculture. So maybe she wasn't being so unreasonable after all.

Once she had dropped the last of the fruit, Zib bent her knees and jumped straight down. She hit the ground laughing, crouching down until her fingers brushed the grass, and bounced back upright with a big grin on her face. "That was fun!" she said. "Are we going to go down the whole cliff like that?"

"I hope not," said Avery, feeling queasy at the very idea.

"No," said Niamh. "The path slopes from here, and we'll be harder to follow when we're moving in and out of the wind like this."

"Oh," said Zib, sounding disappointed.

"Help, please?" The voice was small, piping, and still unfamiliar. All three of them looked up.

The whittled-down Crow Girl was standing at the edge of the mesa, looking uneasily down, an expression on her face that implied she had never contemplated anything she liked less than the idea of jumping to join them.

"I'm too short to fall without hurting myself," she said, somewhat petulantly.

Zib blinked, then frowned. "Can't you be birds long enough to fly down?"

"I'm not sure being birds would be a good idea," said the Crow Girl, and hugged herself. "I think this is part of what it costs, eventually, to be a flock without a heart. The only way I get to be bigger again is if I make or steal more birds to join myself, and they won't have been part of whoever I was before I traded my name away. They won't know how to be *me*. I'm going to wind up turning into somebody else before this is all over, and I don't want it. So I don't want to be birds anymore, not unless I very much have to."

Avery, who had felt the loss of the shine from his shoes as a blow to his very identity, nodded slowly. Even if he assumed the Queen of Swords had told the Crow Girl all the consequences of getting what she wanted, even if he believed she had been honest and upfront, the Crow Girl had lost so many birds—and the memories that they contained—at this point that she was no longer the person who had agreed to pay. She was, in many ways, caught in a bargain she hadn't made, just like any other child. And like any other child, she was afraid.

He stepped closer to the wall, so that he was right beneath her, and spread his arms.

"Sit and push yourself over the edge, and I'll catch you," he said solemnly. "I promise."

She looked at him gravely, as if assessing his

honesty, then did as she was told, sitting and pushing herself away from the edge, eyes screwed tightly shut as she dropped toward him.

Avery caught her and staggered, more from the force of impact than from her weight, which was even slighter than he would have expected from the size of her. He remembered reading somewhere that birds had hollow bones, and supposed she must be proof of it. Stepping away from the stone wall, he set her gently on her feet.

"You can open your eyes now," he said.

She cracked one eye open, and then the other, and beamed at him. "You caught me!"

"I said I would," he said, feeling big and important in that way that only ever came from helping someone else. Seeing her smile at him like that made him feel like he was a hundred feet tall and stronger than any bear. It was an intoxicating sensation. Feeling it, he couldn't understand why anyone would do anything with their lives that wasn't helping other people.

A few feet away, Zib had finished picking up her fruit and was bouncing on her toes, eager to get moving along. "Which way?" she asked Niamh.

Niamh pointed, and they began moving.

It was slow going. The Crow Girl wasn't accustomed to the new length of her legs. Her steps were uncertain and her legs were short; every twenty feet or so, she had to stop for a short rest before she was able to continue on. It would have been frustrating if she hadn't been so clearly making an effort.

Avery's feet still ached, but the warm sunstone followed by the soft, cool grass had dulled most of the pain, and he could even forget how uncomfortable he was from time to time. The path wound gently around the mesa, escorting them toward ground level.

(The word "mesa" can be a confusing one to people who don't live in an area where the hills look like they've been sliced off at the top by a giant's hand. A mesa is a mountain or hill with a very flat place on the top of it, much like a butte, although it's not as funny to say. There are places with lots and lots of mesas, and there are places with virtually no mesas at all. But the mesa is the whole thing, not just the flat place on the very top. So to climb a mountain and find that it has a flat top on it means that you have actually climbed a mesa, and not a mountain at all. Thus the children were descending a mesa, having believed themselves to be climbing up a pathway eaten into the core of a mountain, like a worm eats a tunnel through an apple. The world is made of such contradictory corrections. It would be untrue to fail to place one here.)

Zib gnawed through the leathery skin of her first conconut and munched as they descended, passing another to Avery when he looked at her with evident hunger and silent longing in his eyes. The Crow Girl was missing too many teeth to chew through the skin, and so he split it against the mesa wall, passing her half. Thus fed, they continued their descent.

The whole time, the wind blew. Zib was uncharacteristically quiet. Niamh glanced back at her after their fourth loop around the mesa, and said, "What's wrong?"

"I got us into trouble by talking careless, and I don't want to get us into trouble again, not when we're still not all the way out of the first trouble," said Zib. "And I'm worried about the Crow Girl, and while I'm not going to say that getting away from those people was easy, because it wasn't—it was awful—it wasn't as hard as it felt like it ought to be. Something else is going to happen, and I don't want it to be my fault again."

"Even though it is?" asked Jack mildly, from behind them.

Zib spun around, flinging her half-eaten conconut straight at his head. It hit him on the forehead and bounced off, hitting the ground and rolling to a stop a few feet away. Jack blinked at her, looking startled, and raised one hand to rub the spot where it had hit him.

"Ow," he said, somewhat petulantly. "What did you go and do that for?"

"Stop *sneaking up* on us!" snapped Zib. "All you

people seem to think that suddenly appearing behind somebody and saying 'boo' is just the same as saying hello, and it's not! It's mean, and it's impolite, and it's not fair!"

Jack blinked, looking startled. Avery did the same. Niamh smiled.

"You get used to her," she said to Jack. "Only I hope you won't, because I don't want you to be around enough to do that. What do you want, Jack Daw?"

"Only to upset my mother," he said, amiably enough. He bent and picked up Zib's conconut, lobbing it back to her with a gentle underhand. "Don't throw that at me again. You won't get it back a second time, and I doubt you want to go wishing for more."

"Why would I do that?" asked Zib.

His expression turned almost pitying. "And here I was thinking you were smarter than you looked, even if you're not clever enough to brush your own hair."

Zib scowled at him.

"There's not much for people who can't fly to eat here in the Land of Air," he said. "Mother likes it that way. People tend to have these annoying ideas about staying the way they were born and being human beings for their whole lives, and never being anything else at all. But Mother likes making monsters. It's important to her that she be allowed to make as many as she wants, and that she never runs out of raw materials. So she made farming illegal a long time ago."

"You can't do that!" protested Avery, utterly horrified.

Jack Daw looked at him and cocked his head. "You're a farmer?" he asked. "Spend a lot of time toiling in the fields? Got dirt under your nails?" When Avery squirmed and looked away, he smirked. "Thought not."

"People have to eat, though," said Zib.

Jack shrugged, unconcerned. "They can go to the ocean and fish if they get too hungry, or chew on the grass . . . or come to Mother. She'll always give a hot meal to one of her subjects, or to any traveler who asks her for one. She's happy to share, and her table is always full."

"But there are consequences when you dine with the Queen of Swords," said the Crow Girl, miserably. Her words sounded too old for her childish voice, and matched the sudden deep-set misery in her eyes. She looked away from Jack, out over the grassy fields below them.

"That's true enough," said Jack. "But I think that's so in most worlds, not just this one. You can't sit down to eat at someone else's table and think that the food will be free just because you're not the one who had to cook a single bite of it."

Zib took a step back, away from him. "Why are you here?"

"Oh," said Jack. "Because the Page is distracted right now, trying to wrangle my flock back to the roosts where they belong—two Crow Girls, two Magpie Girls, and one Blue Jay Girl can make a lot of mischief when it suits them to do so, and they don't want to leave when one of their sisters is nearby, dearly in need of birds—and so he hasn't come looking for you yet. But he will, soon enough, and when he finds you, he'll take you to Mother for tea and talking, and then you'll never get back to the improbable road, or find your missing queen. So I'm here to help you."

"*Help* us?" demanded Avery. "Why would you want to *help* us?"

"You're not very clever either, are you, Earth boy?" asked Jack. "I already told your damp girl why I was here, and why I'm here is why I'm going to help, whether you want me to or not. You can't have help without the helper, and you need help sure as anything."

"Why do we need your help?" asked Zib.

"The Page is coming, and he *will* take you to Mother," said Jack. "You can't reason with him. He's been in her service for too long, and all that matters to him now is that he should make her happy, not risk drawing her wrath in his direction. You would make her happy, for a little while."

Zib didn't like the sound of that. She took another

step back, away from the boy, who didn't seem to notice.

"She wouldn't do the same for you, of course," he continued, blithely. "She would make you as sad as she thought she needed to in order to get what she wanted from you. She would make you *miserable*. And then she would make you happier than you had ever once been before, but you would be something other than yourselves if she were to do that for you. You would be remade and belong to her, forever. Even you, drowned girl. There are monsters in the deep, and my mother's creations can thrive anywhere in the Up-and-Under, and even beyond. Your friends could go back to their own world with their hearts cut out of their chests and not have a single difficulty with the transition, if they went to my mother."

Avery opened his mouth to ask another question. Jack fixed him with a withering look.

"But as I said, I am here to help you solely for the sake of annoying my mother, who sometimes feels like being a queen and perfect and beautiful and beloved of almost everything she makes means that she should always get her way, no matter what. It's odd, to think of a parent as being spoilt, but that's what she is: she's spoilt, and it's good for her to not always get her way. If she hears that four children passed through her lands on an adventure and she didn't have at least the opportunity to tempt them with her poisoned fruits, she'll be angry as anything."

Zib, who had been held prisoner by the King of Cups and felt feathers trying to grow through her skin, shuddered at the thought of becoming a monster.

Avery, who wanted nothing as much as he wanted to go home to his parents and his school and his safe, predictable world, shuddered at the thought of becoming something unpredictable.

Niamh, who was already a monster in her own way—people tend to be uncomfortable around dead children, when they understand that's what they're looking at—didn't shudder at all, only watched Jack with silent, measuring eyes.

The Crow Girl turned to him, spreading her arms, and said serenely, "Up, please."

"What?"

"If you want to help us, you can carry me," she said. And it was a logical enough request, a sensible enough approach to the problem of her short legs. She kept her arms up, waiting for him to lift her.

After a beat, Jack stooped and did exactly that, boosting her onto his shoulders and straightening back up again as he gave Niamh a defiant look.

"My girls can't hold the Page forever," he said. "The winds won't tell him where you are if you're with me, because I've asked them not to. As long as you don't attract the attention of any more clouds, you'll be safe."

"Fine," said Niamh. "But you stay on two legs."

"I'll have to, if I want to carry this one," said Jack.

They started walking again, a group of five now, rather than a group of four, with Zib stealing little glances at Jack that made Avery want to scowl and kick the ground. He didn't, though—the grass didn't deserve that kind of abuse—just trudged morosely along, all of them making for the ground, which was still an easy hundred feet away.

They had all started to relax, feeling like maybe they'd be able to navigate this strange and unfriendly land without any more truly major problems, when the wind—which had been blowing steadily and softly since they began their descent—abruptly picked up, blowing harder and harder, until Niamh turned to Jack and shouted, "What's happening?"

"It must be teatime," said Jack. "Mother turns the winds up when it's time to take her tea, to make it harder for the birds to fly, so that all the flocks will come back together into single people and sit down at their tables, and she can feel as if the whole country is having tea together, even when she dines alone."

"Can't you make it stop?"

"I don't control the winds," said Jack. "I can request, cajole, even occasionally command the winds, but I can't *control* them."

Zib, who couldn't see the difference between commanding and controlling a thing, frowned at him as the wind howled around them. "Why not?"

"They don't belong to me," said Jack. "I could command you, if I wanted to, but that wouldn't make you do what I wanted. You'd still be a stubborn, annoying little girl."

The wind blew harder.

"Can't you do *something*?" demanded Niamh.

"I can try." Jack turned his face into the wind and yelled, "Mother! I will not be home in time for tea today! Please stop trying to blow me there on your schedule! I'll stay for dinner if you stop."

The wind died down, long enough for Jack to turn back to them, a pleased, surprised expression on his face, and say, "Well, I didn't think that was going to wor—"

With a sudden roar, the wind gusted hard along the side of the mesa, scattering the children like tenpins off the ledge and out into the open air.

EIGHT

WHERE GRAVITY
MEETS GROUND

Zib's first, stunned thought, before the fear and panic
and need to find a solution to the situation could kick
in, was that this was becoming almost familiar; she
had fallen off of and into so many things since arriving in the Up-and-Under that honestly, the only
surprise was in how long it had taken for *something*
to push them off the mesa, even if she wouldn't necessarily have been betting on an irritated gust of
wind.

Then Jack fell past her, still in one piece, clutching the cowering Crow Girl against his chest, and she
realized that they had much bigger things to worry
about.

"She can't break up!" he yelled. "The wind's blowing too hard! We'd both lose birds if we broke up, and she can't afford to give them up right now!"

Zib blinked before she processed what he was saying. The wind was blowing so hard that if the two of them broke into birds, it would carry at least some of those birds away, and the Crow Girl couldn't lose any more birds if she wanted to stay herself. She looked wildly around, searching the empty air for something that might be able to help them.

There was nothing. They were falling through nothingness, and in another five hundred feet or so, they would slam into the earth, and they would be broken by the impact. This was no welcoming water, no pool of rainbowed mud; this was going to be a hard landing, and they might not walk away.

For the first time in her short life, Zib realized she was something that could die. There had been a world before she existed to be a part of it, and one day there would be a world that came after she'd been a part of it, and she'd be a story for other kids to tell each other at the back of the playground, where all the most delicious stories lingered until every drop of sweetness had been sucked out of them and they were cast aside into boring old history. "There once was a girl named Hepzibah, and then she didn't come to class one day, and we never knew what happened to her," they would say, back in the ordinary town where she had lived until she found the wall into the Forest of Borders; and then they wouldn't say anything else, because there would be nothing else to say.

The thought carried no fear or panic; it was too novel for that, too impossible and new. It couldn't really frighten her before it had time to fully take root and become something true, rather than something surprising and strange. She still flapped her arms a few times, almost experimentally, as if *she* were the one who could break into birds and fly away.

Nothing happened. She hadn't really expected that anything would. She kept falling, tumbling through empty air, toward a ground that was getting distressingly close. She looked around. All her friends—and Jack Daw—were falling with her, and none of them looked like they had any idea how to stop this from happening.

It felt like they were falling very slowly and very quickly at the same time, especially when compared to all the other times that she had fallen off of something, always with a better landing waiting for her at the bottom. And maybe that feeling was true. Feelings could be liars sometimes, could tell you that something was happening when it wasn't, but this was the Land of Air, and the wind had just pushed them off the side of a mesa. Maybe the air was playing with the way they fell, because it wanted to, or because it could, or for no reason at all.

This wasn't how she wanted her story to end. This

wasn't how she wanted any of their stories to end. And so Zib took a very deep breath, and did the only thing she could think of to do:

Screwing her eyes tightly closed, she threw her head back and yelled, into the wind that whipped each word away as soon as it left her mouth, "I *wish* we weren't falling anymore!"

Instantly, they all stopped. It wasn't like being jerked to a halt, and it wasn't like slamming into anything; it was more like the concept of falling had suddenly been forgotten, and they were sinking into the soft embrace of the puffiest featherbed that had ever existed instead. Zib cracked one eye open. Sky above her, gray-streaked and skidded with clouds. She turned her head, and looked down.

Beneath her, instead of grassy field, she saw the white folds and billows of a cloud that was just as soft and warm as she'd always imagined a cloud could be. It surrounded her, holding her up, keeping her from dropping any further. Pushing the heels of her hands against it, she sat up, and the cloud bore her weight.

Looking around, she saw that all her friends had clouds of their own, holding them up. The Crow Girl was still clinging to Jack, her face pressed into his upper arm, shoulders shaking like she was crying. Avery and Niamh were also sitting up on their clouds, and when Zib saw them, she waved.

Niamh waved back, hesitantly. Avery didn't, just dug his fingers into the cloud beneath him like he was afraid he was going to fall right through it and finish his journey to the ground at any moment.

His grip only got tighter as the clouds began to move. They began with a lurch upward, as fast and hard as a carnival coaster, one of those rickety wooden things that smelled like rust and rot and excitement. Zib laughed, the sound half-ripped out of her by the lurching lift in her stomach, and returned her own hands to the surface of the cloud, clutching tight to keep herself from being knocked off. This was better than a roller coaster, and worse, too, because there wasn't a safety harness to take the delicious edge off the danger of it all. So she held fast, and waited to see what the cloud was going to do next.

What it was going to do was leap up another twenty feet or so, until they were almost level with the place where they'd been when the wind first pushed them off the mesa. For a giddy moment, Zib thought the clouds were going to fly them back to level ground. Then the wind pushed against them, still blowing hard, and she realized that it wouldn't matter if they did: the wind would just knock their group off the mesa a second time, and this would all begin again.

So it was almost a relief when, instead of drifting toward the mesa, the clouds took off with an impossible streaking speed, carrying the children away from the mesa, over a rapidly unspooling landscape of green and brown and rocky outcroppings, racing toward some unseen destination. Zib laughed again.

She knew that this was probably terrible somehow. It seemed like all the best things in the Up-and-Under were somehow secretly terrible, hiding their rot deep inside, like apples that had gone bad before you even brought them home, but there were good things here too, and this was a good thing. Even if the ending was bad, a cloud that carried you faster than any roller coaster she'd ever been on was a good thing, and she meant to enjoy it while she could. So she held fast, and she enjoyed it.

Until the clouds began to slow, approaching a solid wall of what might have been smoke or might have been mist, but which she knew, all the way down to the base of her, was just more cloud. The four clouds formed themselves into a loose line, with Avery and Zib at the center, flanked by Niamh, Jack, and the Crow Girl.

"Are you all right?" Zib called to Avery, who was still clinging to his cloud for dear life, and looked like he was considering the merits of being sick to his stomach without knowing what he would be splattering down below.

"That was really, really awful," said Avery. "Don't you think so?"

"No," said Zib, who didn't really see the point in lying, even when they didn't agree. "I thought it was wonderful. I'd do it again, if I didn't think we were about to get into trouble."

Avery shuddered. "Girls are weird."

"Yup," Zib gleefully agreed. "I'm a girl and I'm weird. The Crow Girl's a girl and she's made of birds, and that's weird. And Niamh's a girl, and she drowned and didn't stop moving, and *that's* weird. All the girls we have around here are weird ones."

Avery just shook his head. Jack, meanwhile, was staring at the cloud wall in front of them with something like hope, and something like horror, which was an unusual combination, and didn't bode well for whatever was on the other side.

"What is it?" Zib asked.

Jack looked at her bleakly. "Just try not to argue," he said.

"With who?"

And the wall of clouds began to part. They didn't move the way Zib expected clouds to move, instead pulling apart like curtains, smoothly and easily, staying in two coherent pieces without losing so much as a wisp of vapor. That, alone, told her that these weren't entirely clouds, or weren't only clouds, no matter how much they looked like them. They had to be at least partially something else. There was no other way they could move like that.

On the other side was a wall of mist, blank white and somehow emptier than the clouds had been, blocking out all signs of either land or sky. The clouds carrying the children sailed through the gap as soon as it was wide enough, and Zib twisted to watch as the clouds slammed shut behind them.

Their clouds moved gamely on, heading through the mist like they were on their own version of the improbable road, absolutely sure of their inevitable destination. She turned to look forward again, gripping the cloud to conceal her fear, and realized that she couldn't see Avery or Jack and the Crow Girl anymore; the mist between them was too thick. She might as well have been entirely alone.

She didn't like that. She didn't like it one little bit. And she didn't see anything she could do about it but hold on and find them when this came to an end, whenever that was.

Finally, after what seemed like an eternity of nothingness, they emerged from the blank wall of mist into a bright world filled with sunlight and blue sky, studded by little white puffball clouds like something out of a storybook. Below them was a green grassy field, as featureless and designed for the pleasure of the wind as the field below the mesa had been, and in front of them was another mountain.

This one was high and craggy, a spire of stone stretching endlessly up into the clouds, which clustered around it like the roses around the edges of a wedding cake. Craning her neck back as far as it would go, Zib still couldn't see the top. Past a certain point, it was all clouds and the barest impression of stone. Jack groaned, letting go of the Crow Girl enough to put his hand over his face as their clouds carried them closer and rose higher into the air.

"Where are we going?" asked Zib. She looked down at the cloud beneath her. "I asked you to stop us from falling, you stupid cloud, not to kidnap us!"

The cloud did not stop, or slow, or give any indication that it had heard her. Zib frowned at it. She knew the clouds could understand what she was saying; this one should have listened. It was being rude by refusing, and she didn't like it one little bit.

Up and up they went, up into the clouds, up into the heights, until the ground vanished below them, and there was nothing left in the world but sky, clouds, and the mountain.

It was made of a kind of stone Zib had never seen before, smooth as glass and gray as granite, reflective enough that she could see her own image zipping by as the cloud pulled her ever higher. She began to worry whether there was a place where the air couldn't go. She knew there was outer space up above the world, and she knew that the atmosphere had to run out eventually, but she didn't know when, or even how high they really were.

It was getting colder. She wrapped her arms around herself and shivered, trying to keep her teeth from chattering. It wasn't going to work forever, she knew, but she could usually fool herself into thinking she was warm for a little while if she tried really, *really* hard. And since she was currently riding a cloud up the side of an impossibly tall mountain, she had developed a certain knack for believing impossible things.

Just as quickly as they had started shooting upward, the cloud stopped, jerking to a halt almost hard enough to topple her off the edge. Looking around, she saw that the other clouds had stopped as well, and were drifting closer together.

Bit by bit, they formed into one massive cloud, and the children were together again. Zib immediately stopped hugging her own arms and hugged Avery instead.

"You're shivering," he said.

"I'm cold," she answered.

"I'm sorry," said Avery, and hugged her harder, like he could give her all his own heat. This was a great kindness, for he had nothing else to give. A small thing can still hold great value when it is given freely and there is nothing else to spare or steal away.

The cloud began drifting closer to the mountain, slowly now, almost lazily. Jack twisted to look at the two children, the Crow Girl huddled hard against him. "We're almost there," he said, voice gone tight and low. "She's going to ask you lots of things. Answer honestly, but don't give details. Volunteer nothing. What matters is the fact of the thing, not the reason for the thing. The reason is just a decoration, and she only cares for fripperies when they belong to her."

"Her who?" asked Zib, who was almost certain she already knew, but wanted very, very badly to be wrong.

"My mother," said Jack—and as if that were some kind of password, the cloud spun around and flew as fast as it could toward the mountain.

Just as they should have struck stone, they sailed through it and into a vast cavern that had to be the inside of the mountain itself. The walls here were completely mirrored; Zib could see echoes of them thrown wide in every direction, Zib upon Zib and Avery upon Avery. But in the reflection, Jack and the Crow Girl were both piled-up masses of birds held together by the wires of a silver cage that vaguely followed the outline of the human forms she had expected to see, and Niamh was a pale, waxy dead thing, so clogged with water that she was barely recognizable.

As she registered the depth of the difference in her companions, she realized her own reflection wasn't quite right. Her hair looked like it was on fire, and it was a realistic enough image that she reached up in alarm and patted her head, only relaxing when she felt no heat. Avery's reflection, meanwhile, had skin as faceted as a quartz crystal, catching and throwing back the light. Zib stared. She couldn't help herself. And so she almost missed the other thing the mirrored mountain held.

They were moving, rapidly, toward a castle of white, pearlescent stone, a confection of towers and turrets and high windows. There was no moat, but a ring of storm clouds seemed to fill the same purpose, circling the castle in dark gray that writhed and roiled like the waves of an angry sea. There was nothing beneath the clouds but mountain, and they lashed out again and again with bolts of lightning, striking the stone without visible impact.

The drawbridge began to lower as they approached, dropping to form a safe path over the clouds, into the castle. Zib wasn't even remotely sure that she wanted to go there, but she didn't see how they had a choice at this point. They were even higher up now than they'd been when she called the clouds; if they fell from here, they would die. Maybe not Jack and the Crow Girl, and maybe not Niamh, but her and Avery for sure.

She wanted to be alive more than she wanted to escape the Queen of Swords, and so she just held onto Avery as they sailed forward, over the drawbridge and into the castle.

The room on the other side was grand, with walls of gold and mirrors. These mirrors reflected the way they really were, at least, tangled hair and missing shoes and all. Zib looked around them, trying to see everything at once as the cloud settled to the floor and vanished, leaving them sitting there on the cold marble.

"Here we are," said Jack. He stood, lifting the Crow Girl with him and balancing her upon his hip. She whimpered and pressed her face into his shoulder, clinging to him. The longer she spent without the balance of her birds, the more she seemed to match the child she appeared to be. If she stayed this way for too long, Zib worried they would never get back the girl they knew, and would be babysitting for a stranger instead.

It hadn't been that long since they were children just as small as the Crow Girl was now. But the past, much like the Up-and-Under, is another country, and only the very rarest of children, under the very rarest of circumstances, can find a passport that will take them there. This is for the best, as all who go to the past must return the slow way that the rest of us have already taken to the present, and they will inevitably catch up to themselves. But who knows what changes they might make along the way? Who knows what consequences the trip might carry?

Who knows if they might ever return at all?

For Zib, the years immediately after infancy were a one-way journey the length of a lifetime from where she now stood, in that nebulous age between the playroom and the prom. She wanted her friend back. She wanted to know that she could never suffer the same fate.

But more than anything, she wanted to be back on the improbable road, walking the long, slow way between their beginning and their destination. She stood in turn, and offered her hands to Niamh, pulling the other girl to her feet. They both turned to help Avery up, and the five children huddled together as if for warmth.

Avery looked at Jack and realized he no longer thought of the other boy as an interloper; one fall and kidnapping by clouds had been enough to make him one of them, and now that the line had been crossed, it would not be taken back again. Jack looked back at him, a grimace on his lips and discomfort in his eyes.

"I'm sorry," he said.

"Where are we?" asked Zib.

"My home," said Jack. "My mother's palace."

That was no surprise to hear, however unwelcome it was. He had already told her as much, if less directly. There had really been no other answer he could possibly give. "Oh," said Zib, subdued.

"You know," said Avery. "We've met a King *and* a Queen, and this is the first castle we've seen?"

"That's true," said Zib. She didn't bother pointing out that he hadn't been with her when she met the Queen of Swords; both of them had been there to meet the King of Cups, and she'd come back to him with the skeleton key right after she escaped the Queen, so he might as well have been there too. It wasn't like there was some sort of prize for meeting the most monarchs, especially since both the monarchs she'd met so far had been terrible people.

Castles, though, seemed to be a bit thinner on the

ground than the people who were supposed to live in them. And this castle, grand as it was, wasn't exactly what she would have expected from this particular queen. It didn't seem to have been built with the needs of monsters in mind, for one thing; the doorways she could see were human-sized, and the mirrors, for all that they were infinite, reflected normal things, instead of the distortions of the outside.

Then a stairway unrolled like the tongue of a wolf from the ceiling against one wall, an opening that just kept extending and extending until it touched the ground, red and plush and moist in a terrible way. It was a tongue in all the ways it flexed and bent, but the edges were lined with teeth, sharp as anything she'd ever seen. As she watched, they extended upward into the balusters of a banister. They connected at the top with a railing that grew out of nowhere to join them together. The tongue settled into motionless patience, floor connected to ceiling, monstrous and impossible.

Zib shivered as Avery reached over to take her hand, squeezing her fingers so tightly it hurt. She didn't pull away or ask him to let go. If anything, she welcomed the pain. It reminded her that all this was actually happening, and not something from a story she'd heard once when she was too little to remember. This was real.

A woman emerged from the opening at the top of the stairs and started languidly down, one hand resting on the rail to steady her. Her skin was very pale, with a faint grayish cast, like the Page of Ceaseless Storms, or Niamh; Niamh was more blue than gray, but they could still have been related, however distantly. Her hair was long and white and unsnarled, despite the fact that it hung loose down her back, where it should have been heir to countless tangles. She wore a gown of flower petals and mist, and that was one more thing that should have been impossible but somehow wasn't, because where this woman walked, nothing was impossible.

Avery looked at her and was lost, his eyes going wide and his hand slipping out of Zib's to dangle by his side, even as his mouth fell slightly open. He looked at the Queen of Swords like she was a bowl of ice cream on a summer afternoon or a perfect grade on a math test he'd forgotten to study for, like she was the most impossibly flawless thing to ever have existed in an imperfect world.

"Welcome," she said, in a voice as sweet as the rest of her, and just as perfect. "Welcome, children, to the Palace of Storms in the Land of Air. I have been waiting for you for a very long time indeed."

"Hello, Mother," said Jack. "I have one of your little pets here."

The Crow Girl whimpered again, burying her face in the side of his neck this time, as the Queen of Swords finished descending the stairs and walked, slowly and grandly, toward them.

"I see that," she said. "One of the Crows, isn't it? Crow Girls are so easy to make that I scarcely keep track of them all, and they're flighty enough things that it's best to let them fly away and seek other aviaries when the desire strikes them. Nothing good ever came of trying to contain a Crow who didn't want to be kept. Did I make this one so small?"

"She's lost quite a few birds," said Jack. He gave his mother a challenging look. "The kind thing to do would be to open a cage of blank birds and let her keep the core of herself as it stands. But you won't do that, will you?"

"It's the nature of Crows to be changeable, unless they can be careful," she said, waving a hand, like she was brushing something away. "She'll rebuild her murder the way they all do, with birds who need a flock to belong to, one by one, until she reaches the size that keeps her comfortable."

"Kindness has never been your strong suit, has it?" asked Jack.

"I don't know, my beautiful boy. Did you think it was kind when I pulled your heart out of your chest and built a rookery in its place, a spot for the jackdaws to roost and rest and keep you company? You're never alone, thanks to me. You're not my finest monster, but you're my most precious, and you'll never fly away from me."

"Only because you left me with a name."

"A flock with a name will never roam too far from

home," she said, crisply, and turned her attention on the other three. "A drowned girl, hmmm. Someone else's monster, and not mine, unless I read you wrong."

"No, ma'am, you don't, and I've been here before," said Niamh, shoulders squared in brave, if futile, defiance. "You already know I'm not for you."

"Ah, yes," said the Queen of Swords, with a little moue of distaste. "My Page delivered you to the King of Cups, if I'm not mistaken."

"Not your Page; his," said Niamh. "But yes, I went from your lands to his, and he had the keeping of me until I slipped away."

"Air and Water are close companions," said the Queen, waving the correction aside. She turned her attention to Avery and Zib, gaze sharpening. "You, however . . . you have no feathers, no water in your lungs. Living children. Living *human* children. Oh, you will do nicely."

Her eyes swept over them both, measuring and assessing. Her gaze snagged for a moment on Zib's face, and then she moved on, leaving no sign of recognition behind. Zib exhaled quietly, relieved beyond accounting. She'd been afraid the Queen would remember her as vividly as she remembered the Queen, would mark her in some way as an enemy, and all because she'd screamed when she stepped on a thorn, screamed and troubled a Queen's peace. Some Queens have no right to be peaceful, and so it was with the Queen of Swords, who deserved so much more storm than stillness.

The Queen made a small, noncommittal noise and moved along to Avery, studying him as carefully as she had studied Zib, her head tilted very slightly to the side and a slow smile forming on her lips. "Boy of Earth in the Land of Air," she said, finally. "Oh, I could make such a dust storm out of you. Yes, indeed, you'll do. Jack?"

"Yes, Mother?"

"Put the denuded flock down and come along, we've work to do." She stepped back, spreading her arms, so that the small swords embroidered along the edges of her sleeves hung down straight and free, unencumbered. She carried no weapon; she *was* a weapon, and another would have been more competition more than protection.

"Children," she said. "You are welcome in my lands, for so long as you would care to stay. And I think you'll find you care to stay a long, long time. This can be your home and your haven, if only you accept what it means for you to belong here. Neither of you is opposed to me in orientation; you could be happy in my haven. There will be food to fill your stomachs, and pillows for your head, and I will ask from you the very smallest of payments for your room and board."

Zib glanced anxiously to Jack. He met her eyes and nodded, very slightly. She snapped her gaze back to the Queen before the older woman could notice her distraction and pasted a syrupy-sweet smile on her face, trying to look as if she wasn't so terrified that her skeleton felt like it was shaking inside her skin.

Grabbing Avery's still-limp hand in her own, Zib directed her smile at the Queen of Swords and said, "We would love to be your guests, so long as we can all stay together. Thank you so much, Your Majesty."

The Queen looked at her face and made a tiny sound of acceptance, a deep-throated "mmm" noise. Then she stepped back and clapped her hands together. "Well. You children are quite rumpled from your journeys, and all of you could use a hot bath and a good meal. Jack, please show your new friends to our visitors' quarters. I'll make sure they receive a proper welcome."

She turned, then, and sailed grandly away, back toward her staircase of teeth and tongue, and left the five of them alone.

NINE

GUESTS OF THE
QUEEN OF SWORDS

The staircase Jack used to lead them deeper into the palace was made of marble and gilded wood, and not flesh or teeth or anything like that at all. "Parts of this place come with the land, and they'll pass one day to whoever next wears the crown of Air."

"Won't that be you?" asked Avery, who had the vague idea that the real difference between a King or Queen and a President was whether or not your children eventually got to do your job without anyone else getting a say.

"It might have been, but she cut out my heart and put a birdcage in its place," said Jack, matter-of-factly, like this was a normal thing for a woman to do. They had reached the top of the stairs, and were walking along a corridor lined with portraits of people with very well-brushed white hair. Nothing else about them looked like the Queen of Swords; their skins came in all different colors, although they always had an undertone Avery wasn't accustomed to associating with people, gray or blueish or even one bright, bruised shade of tornado-warning green. "She left me with my name, so I could serve her as a Page, which isn't a position every Court chooses to maintain. I was never a Prince. That isn't how we do things here in the Land of Air."

"Oh," said Avery. He was getting very tired of the way everything he learned only seemed designed to confuse him further, and was starting to suspect that they changed the rules whenever he wasn't looking, twisting them around like threads on a spindle to make sure no one ever really understood.

The hall ended at another stairway, and they began another upward climb. "The Queen *is* my mother, which is unusual; monarchs don't normally have children. They're a conflict with the causes of the crown. For nine months, I made her job difficult to do. I distracted and diverted her, and her advisors had no idea how this was going to change the kingdom going forward. A Queen cannot have a throne divided. So they came to her, and they offered her three choices for the future: She could set the crown aside. She could give me to a passing wind and allow them to carry me away into another future, to be raised from the cradle by some kind soul with gentle hands and nothing else burdening their time. Or she could make a monster out of me. And because she loved me enough to have made me, she chose to keep me with her through the only means she had. I won't ask you to forgive her for what she did. It was terrible and wrong, no matter what her motivations. Every other monster she's made, she's made because they came and asked her to do it."

Avery thought of the Bumble Bear, who had spun them a story of being snatched from his hive without permission either sought or granted, and said nothing. Calling Jack a liar when he was only repeating what he knew seemed like a cruelty, better left to a monster than a boy who just wanted a place to rest his weary face.

"Even me?" asked the Crow Girl, voice unsure. She was walking on her own now at least, matching each of Jack's steps with two of her own.

He looked down at her and nodded. "Even you, button. You came to her, either here or in her protectorate near the Impossible City, and you told her you were unhappy with what you were, and said that you wanted to be something else. She made a Crow Girl of you, so I'm guessing you were a child of fire, and that you told her you wanted freedom for some reason. Fire children and air children make the best birds. Earth and water are less inclined to seek the skies, although both dominions seek a surprising number of Mother's monsters once they've been created."

"I didn't ask to be a monster," said Zib, somewhat dubiously.

Jack glanced back at her. "And see, you're not one. What a victory it must be, not to become what you never asked to be!"

"But the King of Cups put me in a cage, and feathers began to grow beneath my skin."

"The King of Cups is not my mother. He's not my father, either. My father was a tropical storm who blew in on a western wind and stayed long enough to court my mother before he blew away again and dissipated somewhere over the Saltwise Sea long before the day of my birth."

Zib, who had never heard of a woman having a baby with a storm, blinked and didn't say anything. None of the things she had to say felt like they would have moved the conversation forward, and several of them would have held it back.

"He does, however, have certain artifacts that allow him to blend elements. Mother may well have given him that cage to contain his own Crows, and he could have used it in certain ways to make monsters of his own, even if he had little interest in the art. You should be glad you were broken free before it went too far for you to be human again. You would have been an inferior monster if he had made you entirely on his own."

Zib frowned. She wasn't sure that being an inferior monster would have been the problem, when her issue had been the idea of being a monster at all, inferior or not.

She might not have objected, but Avery did. "We don't want to be monsters," he said hotly. "We're Americans, and we want to go home to our families and our houses and our own rooms and our own beds. That means we have to stay children."

"And yet you're accepting my mother's hospitality."

"You told us not to upset her!"

Niamh, who had been quiet since they walked along the hall of portraits, spoke then, and asked, "How much farther to our rooms? We're all very tired, and very hungry, and we don't want to say careless things that might make trouble for ourselves."

All of her companions recognized the warning in her voice, even the Crow Girl, who bit her lip and didn't let go of Jack's hand.

"Not much farther now," said Jack.

"Your mother chose to keep you," said Zib, hesitantly. "Is that why she let you keep your name?"

Jack nodded. "A thing without a name is only and entirely whatever it is in the moment. Your friend is a drowned girl. She's a kind of monster in her own right. But because the Lady of Salt and Sorrow never demands names from her creations, she still knows who she is."

"Death is a kind of transformation, but it answers to no element," said Niamh. "Earth, air, fire, water, aether, coins, swords, wands, cups, alchemy, it doesn't matter: dead is dead and gone is gone, and while the two things aren't always the same, both of them can come for you in any land, regardless of who rules there."

"But I would wager that, if you were to crack her chest, you'd find no heart at all," continued Jack, blithe as anything.

Zib and Avery both looked to Niamh for confirmation, their eyes gone wide with wonder.

Niamh nodded. "My heart was the cost of my awakening," she admitted. "I sank below the waves, and I drowned, and I died, and a beautiful lady with pearls in her hair asked if I was willing to be over, and when I begged her not to let me end, she slipped an eel down my throat to eat the human heart out of me. It's still there. I feel it shift sometimes, when I'm frightened or too far from the water. It will be with me as long as there's a me to be with, and when I end, so will the eel. But it ate my heart. I have no heart left in this world."

"And you kept your name," said Jack, almost triumphantly. "You kept your name, so you're a monster, and you can serve, but you don't belong to anyone. Not the way a heartless, nameless monster does."

"I don't have a heart or a name," said the Crow Girl. "Who do I belong to?"

"You belonged to my mother until she gave you away," said Jack. "Then you belonged to the King of Cups. When you ran from him, you went looking for a new owner. I think you found them." He glanced to Zib and Avery.

Avery looked alarmed. "We don't *own* her. She's our friend, that's all."

"You can't own people," said Zib.

"But she's not people," said Jack. "She gave up being people when she gave her heart and her name away, and now she's something else. Now she's a monster made of feathers and air that looks like a person when she wants to. She has nothing left to give away except for herself."

"So we give her back to herself," said Zib.

"It doesn't work that way," said Jack. "I still belong halfway to myself, because I still have my name."

Half of the things the Crow Girl had done since she joined them suddenly made a horrible sort of sense. Every risk she'd taken, every pair of iron shoes she'd agreed to wear, everything that had gone against her nature as a wild thing, had she only done those things because she thought she somehow *belonged* to them and didn't have a choice? Had they been hurting her this whole time?

"Is there any way it *could* work that way?" blurted Zib.

"You'd have to find her name and her heart before my mother makes off with either one of yours," said Jack, stopping as the hall stopped around them. He gestured to the doors, two on either side of the corridor. "These will be your rooms. Go and make yourselves presentable for dinner, or Mother will send the zephyrs to do it for you." He made this sound like a terrible fate somehow.

Avery stepped forward. "So nothing ate the Crow Girl's heart?"

"Water can do things by brute force all they want," he said, disdain in his voice. "Air is more delicate. We remove things with care, and we keep them safe. Her heart still exists, locked in my mother's vaults, where it stays safe, along with all the others."

Avery and Zib exchanged a look. Then, in unspoken agreement, they turned and opened the doors to the two nearest rooms.

"I'll see you all at dinner," said Jack, and began walking down the hall.

The Crow Girl whimpered and reached for him. He batted her hand away, shaking his head.

"No," he said. "Clean yourself up. Mother doesn't tolerate sloppiness at her table."

And with that, he burst into a flock of gray-crowned birds and flew off down the hall, leaving our four familiar children alone.

"Go to your rooms," said Niamh. "If the Queen of Swords wants us cleaned up for dinner, we'll clean ourselves up. See what you can find. We'll have time to talk later."

She opened one of the remaining doors and went inside. Avery and Zib finally retreated through the doors they had opened, and the Crow Girl was left alone.

She looked at each of the closed doors, tears rolling down her face, and pressed her linked fists against the bottom of her ribcage like she could somehow stop the sinking horror in her stomach. She didn't *want* to be alone. She was a flocking creature, and she had lost so many birds that her body felt like an empty house, all disused hallways and closed-off rooms, familiar and alien at the same time. She didn't feel like she could live there anymore. And now the people who belonged to her flock, the people who should have *known* better . . . those people had left her.

She was still standing there, crying, when Zib's door cracked open and the girl motioned for her to come inside. "C'mon," she said. "You're less of a mess than I am. We should be able to get ready faster together."

The Crow Girl squealed happiness and bolted through the door, into the room on the other side.

And what a room it was! The ceiling was high, painted with a mural of birds and artistically presented winds. Heavy curtains draped the windows, deep blue velvet hemmed in lace and left long enough to brush the floor. The bed was a vast four-poster, surrounded by curtains that matched the windows. Sleeping there would have been like sinking into a cave, all-consuming and all-concealing, as comfortable as a mother's lullaby.

There was a vanity against one wall, next to an open wardrobe, and a smaller room where a bathtub waited, already filled with water topped in frothy bubbles.

"All the clothes are my size," said Zib. "The shoes, too. We should check the room that's supposed to be yours, see if there's anything in there that would fit you."

"Crow girls don't wear clothes," said the Crow Girl. "I have my dress, and that's all I need. Maybe I could rinse the mud off my feet, but we don't wear shoes, either. Not unless we're on a ship or something, and we don't get to have a choice the way we want to."

Zib nodded. "Well, girl-girls wear clothes, and mine are nasty and starting to fall apart. Let's find something I can wear."

Together, they descended on the wardrobe. Most of the dresses were too fancy and frilly for a girl like Zib, who liked things to be as simple as they could be, but some of them were sturdy and looked comfortable. She dug and dug until she found a plain gray dress that would come down well past her knees, making it roomy enough to let her run and jump and climb the way she wanted to, but still dressy enough to hopefully satisfy the Queen. It was the least colorful thing in the whole wardrobe, and so she topped it with a sweater knit from every color of the rainbow, in chaotic splashes of color rather than in orderly lines. She loved it from the moment she saw it.

The Crow Girl was closer to the ground, and so it was easier for her to start digging at the bottom of the wardrobe, where she came up with shoes and socks and underthings. The shoes were too flimsy for Zib's tastes, being slick-soled and strapped on with a buckle, but they were better than no shoes at all, at least for a formal dinner. She clutched her gathered clothing to her chest and turned to look at the bathtub, making a sour face.

The bubbles hadn't gone down at all. The Crow Girl looked at her quizzically. "What's wrong?"

"It's just that I hate baths," said Zib morosely, and walked over to the tub, setting her clothing down on the floor nearby. "Will you help me scrub my back?"

"Sure," said the Crow Girl.

We can leave them there for a time; they do not need observation to take a bath, will do better, in fact, without it, as most children do once old enough not to drown themselves accidentally in the tub. Let us turn our attention, instead, to the others, who have allowed themselves to be isolated, however temporarily.

Avery and Niamh found rooms as perfectly suited to their needs as Zib did, and decorated in similar fashion, although Avery's bed lacked the curtains and canopy, settling for being enormous and invitingly dotted with pillows. Both found baths already drawn and waiting for them, covered in bubbles that smelled of their very favorite things in the whole world. Both found clothing that would fit them perfectly, and carried it with them as they moved to wash the grime of the journey and the salt of the sea away.

Niamh's hair was long, but lacked the autonomy of Zib's. It had never stolen a sandwich or been accused of resembling a hedgerow. She was finished with her bath and toilette long before the other girls. Before even Avery, who had the shortest hair of them all, but spent a large measure of time putting on pair after pair of shoes, watching sorrowfully as the shine faded from each of them.

Zib had traded the shine from the shoes he had been wearing when they climbed over the wall to the Bumble Bear. He had been hoping, in an abstract sort of way, that the reason he'd never been able to get the iron shoes to shine was because iron as a metal didn't care for being polished. Now, though, he had to admit that she had given away something he considered important forever and for always, and would never have it back again.

The world is full of opportunities to give things away, and not half so full of opportunities to get them back again. This is simply and only the way of things, and is neither fair nor unfair, but only inevitable. Some of those things are simple and small—an afternoon, an hour, a thought. Others are vast and insubstantial—a name, a dream, a purpose. Or the shine from a small boy's shoes.

Avery looked at the shoes on his feet, which had been like mirrors when he slipped them on and were now as dull and scuffed as the shoes of a railman, and felt tears burn in his eyes, and felt fury that he'd thought long extinguished bubble in the back of his throat. How dare Zib? How *dare* she?

Rising, he wiped his hand angrily across his eyes and left the room to find the others, dull shoes still on his feet, dull anger bubbling in his chest.

Niamh was standing in the hall. She had slipped plain blue shoes onto her feet, and rinsed the worst of the grime from her body and hair, but her dress was the same, still soaked through and dripping on the floor around her.

"It's not polite to drip all over someone else's house," said Avery, automatically.

"It's not polite to dry a drowned girl, either, and the Queen of Swords knows that; when one rudeness cancels out a larger, more dangerous one, the small rudeness must be allowed to stand," said Niamh.

"Where are Zib and the Crow Girl?"

"In Zib's room," said Niamh. "They're fighting with her hair."

She made it sound like some grand and terrible battle, something that would be a story for the ages, waged without cease until the dragon had been defeated. Avery blinked at her, somewhat taken aback by the gravity of her tone, then twitched toward the door.

She caught his wrist before he could fully turn away. "Give them time," she said. "I don't think Zib wants more company."

The door cracked open.

The Crow Girl emerged first, scaled feet scrubbed clean and feathers shining as Avery's shoes never would. She smiled when she saw the two of them, narrow shoulders sinking with the relief of having her flock back together again.

Zib was right behind her, in her rainbow sweater and her sensible shoes. Her hair, still sopping wet and pulled somewhat straight by the weight of the water, had been combed and detangled until it lay almost flat. It looked dead, like all the life had been pressed out of it. The edges were already beginning to struggle back into curls, and it was clear that once the water was gone, Zib would spring, irrepressibly, back to herself.

Meanly, Avery wondered how she would have felt if, instead of the shine from his shoes, they had traded the curl from her hair. Maybe she would understand how upsetting it was for someone to give away a part of you if someone gave away a part of *her*.

Close on the heels of that mean thought came the guilt, and the understanding that Zib had done what she did to open their path, not to be petty or mean. He didn't want to be petty or mean. He just wanted to shine. Only to shine.

"Where's Jack?" asked Zib.

"He flew away, and he hasn't migrated back yet," said Niamh, waving her hand carelessly. "We need to move along if we want to make dinner without offending the Queen."

"How much do we need to worry about offending the Queen?" asked Zib, as they began to move along the hall.

"Oh, terribly," said Niamh. "This is her land, and her word is the absolute law here. If she calls for someone to be imprisoned, or even executed, they will be. It's almost safer in the protectorates. There, they keep no courts, maintain no castles, and so are more likely to let transgressors move along, choosing to regard out of sight as out of mind. Here, she has a dungeon, and armed guards who will rise to her command if she declares that it should be so. So I would be very careful of offending her during our dinner."

"But what if she wants to make us into monsters?" asked Avery. "What if she says 'I need to hurt you to be happy,' and says that we're somehow the ones who are being unreasonable when we tell her no?"

"You did agree to pay, within reason, when Zib accepted the Queen's hospitality," said Niamh.

Avery shot Zib a sharp look. That was one more thing she'd taken from him: the freedom to leave this place without leaving part of himself behind. She kept *doing* that.

He could see another version of this story, one where he'd climbed the wall alone, one where he'd entered the Up-and-Under on his own. Because this was a story he was telling to himself, and not a life he was trying to actually live, all the inconvenient questions about how he would have survived the trials and tribulations of his journey simply slipped away, replaced by visions of perfect heroism in which he had done the exact right thing at every turn, made the exact right choice at every opportunity, and never taken a single wrong step. Without Zib, he was sure he would have managed to talk his way past the Bumble Bear, but would have done it with the shine on his shoes intact and perfect. He wouldn't have wished for fruit and called down the Page of Ceaseless Storms, or Jack Daw, who he no longer saw as an enemy but still didn't entirely trust, and he certainly wouldn't be caught in the palace of a Queen who might ask anything as payment for her hospitality. He had the distinct feeling that Queens didn't care to be told no when they settled on a price; that if she asked for the thoughts from his head or the sound of his name, he would have to hand them over.

The Up-and-Under seemed far too fond of trading in abstract concepts that didn't actually exist, things that it shouldn't have been possible for anyone, not even a Queen, to give or to take away. And Avery wasn't sure in the slightest how many of those things he had left to lose.

At the end of the hall, a long stairway spiraled down into the depths of the palace. It wasn't the stairway that had brought them here, and they had barely begun to descend it, one step at a time, when the Crow Girl climbed up onto the banister, clasping it between her legs, and slid down into the darkness, laughing raucously as she dropped out of sight.

"Wait—" began Niamh, but it was too late. The speed of the Crow Girl's descent was such that she was too far below them to answer before the question could finish forming. Niamh stared after her for a moment, then hurried after her, leaving Avery and Zib to catch up.

"Are you all right?" asked Zib. "You seem sad."

"I'm not sad," said Avery. "I'm angry."

"Why?"

Avery didn't know how to put all the reasons for his anger, which was sick and curdled and only half-congealed, into words. He was mad because he wanted to go home; he was mad because Zib kept making choices on his behalf. But mostly, he was mad because didn't know how to explain why he was unhappy.

It might seem as if Avery were behaving unreasonably, and in a way, he was; it isn't fair or kind to be angry at your friends when they haven't done anything intentionally wrong, or meant to do you harm. But some harm in this world is not intended, or is done all in innocence, and those who are hurt don't always react in reasonable ways. Zib was a good person at heart, but she was an often thoughtless person at the same time, and she had caused him considerable pain without ever once stopping to ask herself what their injuries meant. So Avery sulked, and they hurried on, chasing the Crow Girl into the depths.

At the bottom of the stairs she tumbled from the banister to the floor, laughing, and Jack Daw was there to scoop her up, an indulgent smile on his face. "It's hard to resist, isn't it?" he asked, conspiratorially. "Mother made a flock of me when I was a little smaller than you are now, and I slid down every banister in this place. She used to make more just to hear me laugh."

The Crow Girl hugged his neck and giggled. He smiled as he slid an arm under her to hold her up, and waited for the others to finish their descent.

The room at the bottom of the stairs was rainbowed like a soap bubble, all iridescence and a delicate dance of endless, swirling colors. There were no windows or draperies, and the marble tables against each wall were laden with recently extinguished candles, their wicks smoking endlessly. The smell was sweet and faintly spicy, and Zib blinked as she stepped off the last stair, inhaling and trying to remember where she'd smelled that smoke before.

"You all look very presentable," said Jack. "Mother will be pleased. She understands that tidiness takes many different forms, even as people do, and 'presentable' for a zephyr isn't the same as 'presentable' for a nixie, but she likes it when people make an effort. Come along, it won't do to keep her waiting any longer than we absolutely have to."

There wasn't any easy way—or reason—to argue, and so they fell in behind him and let him lead them out of the room into a long dining hall in white and slatey gray, the ceiling studded with chandeliers and the floor dominated by a single long table. Avery thought the palace kitchen must be nearby, for the air smelled of every manner of good thing to eat, an overwhelming cacophony of roast meat and vegetables and pastries and sugar. His mouth began to water immediately, as did Zib's. In that moment, he thought he might have been unfair; whatever the Queen wanted them to pay to feast by her side, it would be worth it, and utterly reasonable for what they were going to receive.

The Queen herself was seated at one end of the

table, wearing a new dress, dark blue as the sky after an evening thunderstorm, and struck through with jagged lines of silver embroidery, like lightning. It seemed like a stretch to Avery to grant lightning to the Queen of Swords; it wasn't air, it was electricity. But as this place's definition of "air" seemed to include storms of all kinds, it didn't feel worth mentioning.

"Hello, children," she called, sweet as anything, a smile on her face. "Come and join me. We have so many wonderful smells to feast upon."

Avery's stomach growled. He walked toward a chair, and sat, only blinking a little when he saw that there were no plates, and no forks or knives or other things to eat with. He turned bemused eyes on the Queen of Swords, who laughed.

"Oh, child, no," she said. "Don't look at me so, with hope and hunger in your eyes. We'll fix both those things soon enough. But there's nothing to be eaten here. My table is not for feasting. What a curious thing that would be, to prepare such delicious smells and repay them by treating them like grist for the mill!"

"Mother, you promised them hospitality," said Jack, setting the Crow Girl into a chair of her own before taking a seat beside her. "They're creatures of flesh and substance, even the damp one. Creatures of flesh and substance can't subsist on scent alone."

The Queen frowned petulantly. "They can if I say they can."

"No, they can't," he said, tone gentle. "No more than I could."

"You don't dine at my table!"

"Not often, and not since you made a flock of me," he said. "You gave me wings so I could truly belong to your country and never claim your crown, and I love your land and have no care for your crown, so you got what you wanted, and I fill my stomachs on all the little things that jackdaws can desire. I eat elsewhere."

The Queen blinked, looking around at all the children. "Is this what you all want?" she asked.

They nodded in ragged unison.

She scoffed. "Fine," she said, snapping her fingers. A wind blew through the room, depositing plates, knives, and forks in front of each of the children. "But don't you complain to me if someone else swallows something you wanted to get a better sniff of."

She snapped her fingers again, and a second, stiffer wind blew through the room, this time dropping trays and platters and vast bowls and woven baskets of every sort of good thing imaginable on the long length of the table. Steaming hot rolls dripping butter and honey, roast chicken and beef and fishes from all the rivers in the world, sliced fruit and cheese and cold salads and hot vegetable dishes. A casserole easily as large as a Thanksgiving turkey landed in front of Zib, steaming and smelling of oyster stuffing and celery and spices, like a little piece of her grandmother's kitchen brought before her.

And then there were the drinks! Pitchers and bottles and tureens, filled with liquids in every color, some of them fizzing and effervescing into the air, tiny bubbles rising to the surface to burst from the sheer excitement of being. Others were cool and calm as drinks normally were, everything from milk and water to fruit juices, coffee, and tea. Zib made a small sound of delight. Even Avery smiled, reaching for a particularly succulent-looking platter of roast scallops.

The Queen of Swords leaned back in her chair and folded her arms as the children began piling things onto their plates, a pout on her face and a stormy expression in her eyes. Only Jack didn't reach for any of the food, but smiled sweetly at his mother.

"It's very kind of you to take the physical needs of people less advanced than your glorious self into account," he said. "I know how hard it can be to remember how limited they are, and it's the mark of a truly generous queen to take steps to keep them comfortable despite their frailties."

"It is, isn't it?" asked the Queen, pout fading slightly as she sat up straighter and unfolded her arms. "This is an act of generosity and kindness, and nothing more. Why, they should give me the throne at the top of the Impossible City as soon as they admit that their precious Queen of Wands has flown the coop and won't be coming back to them. The rotation says it should go to the King of Cups next, but we all know he'd make a terrible monarch of us all. Too distracted, too sleepy. The Up-and-Under needs dynamism and change! That's why we went for fire in the first place. Let air take our turn."

So the Queen of Swords did know that her fellow queen was missing, and it wasn't any sort of a secret they would have to try to keep from their host. Avery relaxed, sliding a slice of chicken pie onto his plate next to the scallops. He'd been afraid of keeping secrets from a queen.

She turned her attention on him, as if summoned by the lowering of his guard. "You've given something to one of my monsters," she said. "I can see it on your skin, but I can't quite catch hold of what it was. What have you given away?"

"The shine from my shoes," he said, voice dropping into resentment by the end of the statement. "And *I* didn't give it away. Zib gave it away for me, to get us past your Bumble Bear."

"He was a fine piece of work, and no mistake about that," said the Queen, a wistful smile on her lips. "He started as a bee, not a bear, and only one of those. It's a fine act of transformation to take something so small and temporary and make it over into something so very large and lasting. He'll live centuries, my Bumble Bear, long after all the beehives in all the meadows in the world have gone to dust and decay, into distant days when the fields are pollenated by children holding paintbrushes in each hand."

The image managed to be charming and horrific at the same time, which was no small trick. Avery blinked.

"I didn't do it to be mean," said Zib. She sounded hurt, and her eyes were on Avery as she spoke. "He was going to gobble us down, or not let us pass, or both, if we didn't give him something, and it was just the first thing that came into my head."

"It was *mine*," said Avery. "It was mine, and I miss it. I want to shine and I *can't*. You could have given away something that was yours."

"I'm sorry," said Zib. "I would have, if I'd been thinking faster, and if I hadn't been afraid of being eaten."

"You could give away something of yours now, to pay your stay for the night," said the Queen of Swords. "Anything you'd like, as long as it's yours, and not anyone else's. Give me your name, or your heart, or your left thumb. Whatever you want."

Zib blinked at her, eyes gone wide and round. "I . . . I don't *want* to give away any of those things."

"You agreed to pay for my hospitality, though," said the Queen. "You'll have to give me *something*, or you'll be a liar, and I can take whatever I like from liars." The threat there wasn't even very veiled.

Zib glanced, frantically, to Jack and Niamh,

waiting for one of them to say something terribly clever that somehow saved her from the consequences of her own actions. Neither of them met her eyes. She looked back to the Queen of Swords.

Zib was not a bad child. She was thoughtless sometimes, but who among us hasn't been? Who among us hasn't said something hurtful in the heat of the moment that we came to regret later, when we saw how it had wounded the people we adored? Who among us hasn't broken someone else's toy or eaten someone else's favorite snack, or even gotten a treat that someone else was begging for? Thoughtlessness is not a crime, but a thing doesn't need to be a crime to come with consequences.

Taking a deep breath, Zib faced her own. "Anything, you say?"

"Anything."

"Can I give you my freckles?"

"You can," said the Queen, and looked so unaccountably pleased that for a moment, Zib wanted nothing more than to change her answer, to say that no, her freckles were something she could never give away or spare, even for an instant. How could a freckle be given, or taken, after all?

But instead, she ducked her head a little lower, and said, "Then you can have them. For your hospitality, and for letting us stay here."

"Thank you, child," said the Queen, smile returning to her face. "I call this a fair trade, if a somewhat smaller one than I would usually agree to, but this is the land of transformation and transmutation, and you bargain fairly."

"Not transmutation," said Jack.

"I'm sorry?"

"This is the land of transformation," he said. "I will absolutely agree to that. But transmutation is the domain of fire, and you can't claim what isn't yours."

"Jack, don't talk back to your mother," she said, sharply.

"I'm not talking back, I'm disagreeing with something factually incorrect," he said. "There's a difference."

"I don't think so," she said, and stood. "I tire of this meal, and your company. When you finish feasting, you may return to your rooms, and sleep safely until the morning. Breakfast has also been paid for by your friend; be grateful to her. When you wake, we can discuss the cost of safe passage through my lands, and whether it's a thing you'd even want to have."

"I thought . . ." Zib paused, swallowing. "I thought safe passage was included in hospitality."

"It might have been, if I were feeling generous." The Queen smiled abruptly, baring her teeth like a wild thing, so that Zib shrank back in her seat. The Queen rose, still smiling that terrible smile. "I don't feel very generous toward the girl who traded screams for a skeleton lock when she could have bartered fairly. Sleep well, children. All of you. I'll see you in the morning."

She swept from the room then, leaving them looking after her—all save for the Crow Girl, who was eating as steadily as anything, shoveling food into her mouth with both hands. She paused, swallowed, and looked around at the others. "What's wrong?" she asked. "This is good. You should try some."

"What did she mean about the smells?" asked Avery, trying to break the tension, at least a little bit.

"This is the Land of Air," said Jack. "We own little of substance here, for Air must remain ephemeral, or it ceases to be itself. Even our borders are likely to shift in the night, although some aspects of them hold steady. The beach where you first arrived has been ours for many years, for example, and seems set to remain ours for many more."

"Oh," said Avery. He was doing his best to sound as if he understood. He was, unfortunately, failing.

Jack smiled. "Because we are ephemeral, ephemeral things belong to us," he said. "Sounds and scents first among them. We grow very little here, as the wind makes it all but impossible for soil to hold a seed, and so there's never enough for the animals to eat. But we have all the smells of all the good things in the world, and we have chambered caverns where all the whispered secrets anyone has tried to hide echo until someone comes to catch them. We have palaces of prophesy and cities of song, and we find that we don't much miss the solidity of the Earth, or the fluid constants of the Water. We have what we need."

"We can't survive on only smells," protested Zib.

"Not yet you can't," said Jack. "Only wait, and linger long enough, and you'll find yourself quite able to feast as one of us does, and not as a child from your world does at all. Just offer Mother your appetite the next time she asks for payment, and you'll find yourself more than able to quell your hunger on the smell of food, and your thirst on the sound of water. It might serve you well, later in life, to never need to stop what you're doing to search for food, to never need to waste a wish for an armful of fruit."

Zib's cheeks burned red, freckles standing out like brands against her embarrassed flush. She stood. "I think I'm not hungry anymore," she said, stiffly. "Is there a shorter way back to our rooms?"

"Distance is a solid thing," said Jack. "It only applies here when Mother wants it to."

"So that means yes?"

"It means if you follow Mother out the door, you'll be back where you want to be," said Jack.

"I highly doubt that," said Avery stiffly.

Zib snorted, rose, and walked away, following the trail struck by the Queen of Swords to and through the door. When she stepped through, she disappeared, and the other four were left alone.

Avery and Niamh exchanged a look. Niamh

shrugged. "We don't know when we'll get fed again," she said. "We may as well eat."

Avery nodded his agreement, and the children resumed their supper, and except for the absence of Zib, everything seemed to be normal, for a time.

TEN

JARS UPON JARS OF HEARTS

The door deposited Zib in the hallway where her bedroom was located, and she landed there alone. With no one to hurry her along, she lingered to look at the portraits, trying to see some commonality between the Monarchs of the Air.

There were none. Their skins had inhuman, clouded undertones; their eyes were filled with storms. Nothing else about them seemed to be shared, nothing else about them seemed to be steady from one onto the next. Last in the line was the Queen of Swords as they knew her, smiling at the painter who had done her portrait, a baby who must have been Jack painted, sleeping, in her arms.

"She whisked the air away from me so I would fall

asleep during portrait sessions when I was young," said Jack, from behind her. Zib gasped and spun around. He smirked at her, raising one hand in a small wave. "Hello."

"What are you doing here?" she asked.

"Well, my mother owns the palace, so I thought I was allowed to see her guests to their rooms," he said. "Do you object?"

"I left you with the others," said Zib.

"Ah," said Jack. "Well, you see. My mother is very protective of me, and wanted to be sure that no matter what happened, I would always come home to her. Not like her Crow Girls, who go away all the time, and often don't come back to her at all. They're discrete flocks, you see. Put three Crows in a room, you'll have three murders."

"What if I put three jackdaws in a room?"

"In the Land of Air, that's not a thing that can be done," said Jack. "There's only one Jackdaw, and only one Jack Daw, and every corvid in my clade is a part of my clattering."

Zib blinked. "You mean you're *all* the jackdaws?"

"I am," said Jack. "I can be in as many places at one time as I'd like to be, and right now, I'd like to be at dinner, and I'd like to be here with you."

"Isn't it confusing?"

"It can be, but mostly it's not." Jack shrugged. "I don't know what the other Jacks know until they come back to the flock and we trade birds between us. But once that's done, all of me will know what any of me knows. It keeps things simpler."

"Oh," said Zib. She didn't see how this was keeping things simple, even a little bit. It seemed more like it was making things ever more complicated. Then: "Wait, your mother took away your air when it was time for pictures? Wasn't she worried about hurting you?"

"Oh, she took it away for too long, several times, and then she had to breathe me alive again," said Jack, almost carelessly. "It loosened my heart in my chest—dying always does—and so it was easier for her when she needed to slice me open and break me into birds. There was never a chance that she was going to hurt me."

Zib shrank away from him, a frightened smile on her face. "Well, thank you for coming to see me."

"These pictures always fascinated me when I was a kid," said Jack. "Art can be so *meaningful*, don't you think? Some things are symbolism, but other things are secrets. If I wanted to look for a secret, I'd look for what all the pictures had in common."

"What?"

"Good night, Hepzibah." Jack broke into birds and flew away, cawing and calling between the pieces of himself.

Shaken, Zib watched him go before turning and slipping back into her room.

The bed seemed suddenly incredibly inviting. She

stepped out of her shoes as she made her way over to it, falling face first into the pillows and closing her eyes. The wind whistling outside the windows sounded like home, sounded like singing, sounded like the hum of her father's radio, the one he liked to listen to before dinner.

Zib tumbled into sleep without really noticing, and while she was there, she had the strangest dream:

The Queen of Swords came into her room as a puff of smoke that quickly knit itself into the shape of a woman, standing next to Zib's bed and looking down on the sleeping child. In one hand, the Queen carried a small basket, and even though Zib was asleep, eyes closed, she could see that it contained all the sort of little things that Zib's mother took to the bathroom with her in the evenings, the ones she kept on her bureau in the bedroom, away from her daughter's over-eager little hands.

"Sleep," breathed the Queen, and Zib settled even deeper into the bed, more tired than she could ever remember being in a dream. Normally, dreams were where you went to be wide awake and full of energy, even after the very longest days. But right now, the thought of even keeping her eyes open made her feel like she never wanted to wake up, ever again. So she closed her dream eyes, and because this *was* a dream, she could still see the Queen standing over her. Could see as the Queen pulled a bottle of lotion out of her basket, and a soft cloth with it, and leaned over to begin dabbing lotion onto Zib's skin.

It smelled of lemon and roses. It smelled like a sweet summer treat, something delicious to be shared out at a picnic. Zib inhaled the scent and relaxed even more, sure that nothing that smelled so incredibly nice could ever be used to hurt her.

The Queen rubbed the lotion into every inch of Zib's exposed skin, stopping only at the lines of the girl's dress. She tugged, somewhat experimentally, at the cuff of one sleeve. "Wouldn't you sleep better without this?" she asked, in a cajoling tone.

"My mother says good girls always sleep with nighties on," said Zib, in the distant, dreamy voice of the deeply sleeping, the smell of lemon and roses in her nostrils.

The Queen hissed between her teeth. "Very well," she said, and rubbed the last of the lotion into a patch on Zib's arm. "When payment is requested again more quickly than you think is entirely fair, remember this moment, and settle your debts."

She put the cap back on her bottle, replacing it in the basket, and began wiping the soft cloth she carried across Zib's exposed skin. It was softer than springtime sunlight, softer than a light rain on an April morning. It felt like mist, like a murmur, and when it was gone, Zib wanted to ask for it to come back again. But she couldn't move. The weariness had her, pulling her deeply down, keeping her pinned and prisoned in the cradle of her bed.

Something was wrong with that. She didn't like it at all. But she liked the lotion and the cloth so very much that it didn't seem to matter as much as it should have, and so she sighed and settled deeper still, eyes still closed.

She heard, rather than saw, the satisfied smile in the Queen of Sword's voice, as the woman bent and pressed a kiss to her forehead. "Rest well, Hepzibah Jones, and remember this when you wake: all debts can be settled forever and for always if you'll give me your heart, or your name. Those are the treasures past all price. You could stay here forever if you gave me one of those, and owe me nothing for the pleasure. Remember."

Then she was gone, and Zib sank down into dreaming, and knew nothing more until the morning, when the sound of birds outside the window woke her. They were yelling gleefully at one another, a glorious cacophony better than any alarm clock, and she sat up with a mumble of discontent, rubbing her eyes.

The smell of rose and lemon hung lightly in the air. That explained the dream she was sure she'd had the night before, because why would the Queen of Swords have been in her room?

Rising from the bed, she moved toward the water closet, where she did her business and picked up the toothbrush that had been set out for her use, turning her attention to the mirror.

Then she screamed, loud and shrill as anything.

She was still screaming when the door to her room banged open and Avery and Niamh came rushing inside, following the sound of her distress. "Zib!" shouted Avery. "Are you all right? Are you—oh."

For he had just seen her as she turned away from the mirror, and he couldn't think of anything else to say.

Niamh didn't say anything at all, only looked at Zib with eyes gone wide and grave. But when Zib started to turn back to the mirror, Niamh was there, grabbing her arm, stopping her. "It won't do you any good to see that," she said, voice low. "It won't change anything. Let it be. You made your bargain. You paid your debts."

"But . . . but I said . . . I only said she could have my freckles," said Zib, the fine edge of hysteria in her voice. "I didn't say she could . . . I didn't say . . ."

And with that, she whipped back around to the mirror despite Niamh's restraining hand, staring at her unfamiliar reflection.

Not completely unfamiliar: her hair was the same, wild and uncontained and curling madly, and her face was the same, features drawn with the lines she had known for her entire life. It was only the color of her that had changed.

Zib's had always been a comfortably deep tan,

sunbaked and well-weathered, the color of new-dried leaves or well-cooked but unburnt toast. Now she was white in a way no person was meant to be white, whiter even than Eloise Morris, who had what Zib's father called "the albinism" and was so pale she could burn on a cloudy day if she even looked outside. No, Zib was white like a sheet of paper was white, like the snow was white, like people were never, ever supposed to be.

And her freckles were gone. Every single one of them, even the tiny one next to the corner of her mouth that her mother used to say was a lockbox for all the kisses she was ever going to give when she got older. Those kisses had been stolen now, snatched away by the Queen of Swords, along with all the color she had ever known or possessed. She could feel the blood burning in her cheeks, roused by her distress, but it didn't show in her cheeks, which remained as bleach-white as a swan's feathers. Tears rose in her eyes.

Niamh settled a hand on her arm. Zib managed, barely, to resist the urge to shake it off.

"There are always risks when you bargain with the creatures of the air," she said, voice low. "I'm sorry. But this changes nothing. We need to find a way out of here, and we need to find the Crow Girl's name and heart if we can, or she'll be someone else entirely once she's gathered enough birds to be herself again."

Zib turned away from the specter in the mirror, no longer able to bear the sight of herself. "I'll get dressed," she said.

"We'll wait outside," said Avery.

He walked out of the water closet, Niamh beside him, and neither of them spoke until the bedroom door was safely closed behind them. Then he turned toward her and asked, voice low, "Did you know the Queen would do this? When Zib offered her freckles, did you know?"

"No," said Niamh. "The people of my city consort mostly with our own kind, and with the Lady; when we must make bargains with the other monarchs, we prefer the King of Coins, for mud stands between the borders of our lands, and belongs to both his people and ours in equal measure. I knew the Queen was wicked and tricky, but I had no idea this was the form her trick would take. Freckles seemed like such a small thing to sell . . ."

"I don't think anything is small here," said Avery grimly, suddenly very aware of how easily selling the shine from his shoes could have gone terribly wrong.

They had gotten lucky, once. And luck didn't seem to be in high supply in the Land of Air.

"No," said Niamh.

The door opened. Zib slipped out, still white-faced, but dressed and ready for the day ahead. "Where do we even start looking?" she asked.

"Where the wind won't go," said Jack Daw, from

the other side of the hall. All three children gasped and spun around to see him leaning against the wall, as careless as a question, hands tucked down into his pockets. He looked at them, almost amused, eyes catching longest on Zib. "So she's planning to make a jay of you, then. It makes sense, I suppose. She has as many crows and ravens as a rookery can hold, and she's not in the market for magpies or jackdaws at the moment. You'll make a fine blue chatterer, once she splits you into a scold."

"I won't be anything other than myself for her, or anyone else," said Zib stiffly. "What do you mean, where the wind won't go?"

"This palace belongs to my mother, and it's full of birds and breezes," said Jack. "We go where we like, and we do as we like, and she makes little enough move to stop us, for both birds and breezes thrive best when they fly free. But there are places where the wind won't blow. If you can find a way to find them, you can find my mother's secrets."

Zib frowned, and was still frowning when Avery snapped his fingers and said, "We need a candle. Jack, can you tell us where to find a candle?"

"I suppose you'd like a flame as well?" asked Jack. "If you go back to your room and open the top drawer of the writing desk, you'll find candles enough to light a banquet, and matches beside, that you might make use of them properly. Why?"

But Avery was already running back into his

room, leaving the others standing in the hall and watching after him.

He returned after a moment, a box of matches in one hand and three candles in the other. He handed a candle each to Niamh and Zib, who accepted them with perplexed expressions on their faces, and struck the first match.

"I'm sorry I didn't get you a candle," he said to Jack, as he applied the match to Niamh's wick. "But the Crow Girl hasn't gotten out of bed yet, and I need you to stay here so she won't be frightened when she wakes up all alone. Please."

"Birds of a feather, and all that," said Jack. He glanced at Zib. "We look out for each other, once we find our wings."

Zib held her candle out to be lit, eyes on Jack. "I don't want wings," she said. "I want to go home and see my mother and father, and to look normal again, the way I'm meant to look, not the way I am right now. This isn't right for me. Eloise is supposed to be paler than a promise. I'm not."

"Then I hope you find where the winds don't go," he said.

Avery lit her candle, and the shadows it cast on her bone-white face were like living bruises, stark and terrible. Zib took a step back as Avery lit his own candle and shook the match out.

"Fire bends away from wind," he said, holding the candle up so that his words made the flame flicker and dance. "If the wind blows everywhere in this castle except the place where the winds don't go, then the candle flames will only be still when we find that place."

It sounded ridiculous and clever at the same time, the way the best ideas always did. Niamh and Zib nodded, and Jack waved, and the three travelers began to move, slowly, through the palace of the Queen of Swords.

Niamh had traveled along two halls when a bird suddenly cawed at her from a windowsill and she jumped, dropping her candle. It extinguished when it hit the floor, and she straightened, looking sorrowfully at the darkened wick. Whatever there was to be found, she wouldn't be the one to find it.

Avery and Zib walked in opposite directions, both exquisitely aware of just how alone they were, and just how vulnerable. This was the home of the maker of monsters, and both of them had lost something due to her art; if they weren't careful, they had so much more to lose. So many things that they had never considered possible to take away were at risk here, and so they moved as quickly as they dared, candles in their hands and slow dread growing in their hearts.

Avery turned a corner and found himself in front of the Queen of Swords herself, dressed in a beautiful gown of clouds and shadows, her hands tucked into her sleeves and an indulgent smile on her face. She looked down at him.

"Avery, excellent," she said. "I was hoping we would have the opportunity to talk without your little friends or my meddling son. Will you walk with me?"

"I . . . Yes." There was no polite way to refuse her, and Avery had been raised to be a polite child. Even as every nerve he had shrieked "danger," he found himself falling into step beside her.

"Quite a dangerous thing, a little flame," said the Queen, gesturing to his candle as she led him along the hall. "Did you know that fire can't exist without air? Because it's quite true! Cut a flame off from the air around it and it withers and dies in an instant, extinguished." She reached over then and pinched out the candle flame, snuffing it neatly between her fingers. When she pulled her hand back, smoke drifted lazily upward from the wick, seeking the ceiling. "You could light it again, but it would be a different flame now. Fire is so transitory. I suppose that's why it trades in transmutation, not transformation."

"I don't understand the difference," said Avery.

"I'm sorry," said the Queen. "How rude of us, not to see how ignorant you are! Travelers from other countries are almost always ignorant in the beginning. It comes of passing through the Forest of Borders, which doesn't like people who know too much. The truly clever see a wall that doesn't belong somewhere, and they think to themselves, 'I should find an adult,' not 'I should climb over this and see what's on the other side.' So only very ignorant and foolish children come from your country to the Up-and-Under, and both those things can be resolved, if someone takes a patient hand and the time to do the fixing. Ignorant is a solvable condition. Foolishness solves itself, given time and suffering enough to ground a person on solid footing."

"Isn't air a flighty thing? Shouldn't you be against grounding people?"

"Air is fickle, but a monarch must be steady," said the Queen of Swords. "No one is ever entirely a single thing on their own, not even the keepers of the quarters. Your Lady of Salt and Sorrow, for instance. Sorrow is a watery emotion, and serves her place well. Salt, however, comes from stone and sand and enters the sea, where it lingers in suspension. So she is a creature of water *and* earth. I am the Queen of Swords, and swords, while they stand for air, can be made from all manner of things. So all four elements walk in me."

"Oh," said Avery, not quite understanding.

The Queen laughed like a ringing bell. "It's all right, child, no one will blame you for being a little bit confused. It's all very confusing. There are people who study their lives away without ever quite understanding the subtle ways that things are woven together, and others who spend those lives trying to purify the elements, in themselves, or in their passion projects. A woman entirely of air would be unable to hold a thought from one second to the next, worse than a Crow Girl, scattered as a starling. And a boy entirely of earth would be unable to change his mind ever, no matter what he saw or experienced or learned about the world around him. He would be static and stuck in the moment of his creation. So tell me, boy made of mostly earth, is that a fate you would wish or want for yourself?"

"No," said Avery, who still didn't quite understand, but knew the proper answer all the same. Any time someone asks if you want a fate for yourself that doesn't involve a thousand soft pillows or a million servings of ice cream, the answer is very likely to be no. He shook his head in illustration. "I like learning things and growing better than I was before I knew them."

"Very good," she said. "Now, where are your friends? It's time for breakfast, and for paying your second day's stay . . ."

"I don't know," he said, in all honesty. "We split up back by our rooms."

"Then it seems we must go looking. You'll come along, of course. It wouldn't do to lose you in the process of finding them."

And she turned and walked off down the hall, and Avery had little choice but to follow, a feeling of hopeless helplessness growing in the pit of his stomach, which was empty of all breakfast, and so had plenty of room for holding dread.

On the other side of the palace altogether, Zib walked cautiously along another hallway, her candle still lit and held in front of her, eyes locked on the flame. Her surroundings didn't matter as much as every little twitch and flicker of the fire in front of her, which reacted to every small wind blowing through the palace.

A few times, it seemed as if the wind blew so strongly that the candle had to go out, but she shielded it with her hand until it steadied, and kept moving, deeper and deeper into the palace, until she reached a corner where the flickering stopped entirely. Zib stopped as well, blinking at the suddenly steady flame of her candle.

She moved closer to the wall. The flame didn't flicker. She took two big steps back, and the flickering resumed.

This time, when she moved closer to the wall, she didn't stop until she was right up against it. Leaning closer, she saw a thin line, like a scratch in the wallpaper, or a seam, running from the floor to a point above her head.

It was like so very many things, and it was also like a door.

This is why it was important for Zib to be the one to find the place where the wind didn't blow, and not one of her companions. Much as every person carries one element or another nestled like an unhatched egg beneath their breastbone, holding and defining who they will become, every person has a weed planted in their heart when they are born. The name of this weed is "curiosity," and in some it only sprouts a little, while in others, it finds wonderfully fertile soil.

Niamh's weed had frozen long ago, stopping its growth when it was barely more than a sprout. Avery's had never been nurtured. But Zib's was a flower in full bloom, fruiting and glorious, and so when she saw how that seam resembled a door as much as it did anything else, she pressed her palm against the center of it and pushed inward. It was a thing her companions would not have thought to do.

It was also, in this instance, correct.

The rectangle cut from the wall shifted slightly, sliding inward, until there was a click and it slid aside, revealing a dark corridor set into the wall itself. It would have been terrible to walk without a light.

But Zib was carrying a candle.

She stepped fearlessly into the dark, and her candle illuminated the walls around her, showing the shape of a narrow hallway. She walked along it to a winding stairway, spiraling down into the deeper dark. That *did* make her pause, if only for a moment, before she started heading carefully down, taking her time with each step, to be certain of her footing.

Behind her there came a click, as the door slid closed. Zib took a breath and kept going, until she reached the end of the stairs.

Not far away was another door, the edges etched in light. She moved toward it, and her questing hand found the knob. A twist, a turn, and the door was open, revealing a room, wider than the hall, but longer than it was wide, lit by bright white illumination with no visible source, and lined with shelves.

Each shelf was heavy with jars. Clay jars, glass jars, even a few jars that looked to have been made of stone. Zib stepped inside, and the door swung shut behind her, but the flower of her curiosity was urging her on, and she barely noticed.

Picking up the nearest jar, she turned it in her hand and, on the back, found a label: *MEGAN*, it said.

Holding her candle carefully, she used her arm to brace the jar against her body and unscrewed the lid, peeking inside.

Then she screamed, very nearly dropping the jar entirely. She *did* drop her candle, which went out when it hit the ground, and used her suddenly free hand to slam the lid back down over the jar's lid, breathing heavily, unable to forget what she had seen.

Inside the jar was a still-beating human heart.

ELEVEN
DOUBTS AND DANGERS

There were so many jars. It felt like there were as many jars as there were stars in the sky, and every one of them held a beating heart. Every one of them was someone the Queen of Swords had whittled down to nothing, one small debt or bad bargain at a time, until she had made a proper monster out of them, and turned them loose on the world as a Crow Girl or a Bumble Bear or whatever else happened to take her fancy.

Zib knew even without trying that she couldn't possibly carry so many jars, and so she settled for moving among them, reading the names written on their surfaces. None of those names meant anything to her. She couldn't have guessed which one had belonged to the Crow Girl if she had been dared to, and had no idea what would happen if she guessed it wrong. Still, it felt important to look at all the names, and so she did, one after another, until she found a jar with no name on it at all.

Jack had been allowed to keep his name and not his heart. This jar, she tucked under her arm as she walked back to the door to the stairs. She would have to climb them in the dark, but that was fine; she had stairs in her house at home, and she went up and down those in the dark all the time. If she just kept her eyes closed, she could pretend that she was sneaking back to her bedroom after a midnight trip to the kitchen for a glass of water and a piece of cheese. It would be fine. She wouldn't fall.

She didn't fall. Zib slipped out of the room of jars and padded silently down the dark hall to the winding stair, climbing with her eyes safely closed, so that there would never be any question of whether she could see where she was going. At the top of the stairs she stumbled a little, making the transition to level ground, and continued onward to the door.

That was where she felt her first real twinge of fear, because the door was closed. That was also when she realized that she'd left her extinguished candle behind. It was possible that the Queen might not notice a single jar missing, out of so very many, but the candle would be discovered for sure. She would realize someone had been inside her private space. She might start looking to see if anything had been touched or taken. She might get mad. She might—

Zib's fumbling fingers found a handle on the inside of the door. She pushed it down and the door swung open, and she staggered out into the light.

It was no brighter than it had been before she went into the wall and the places beyond, but it seemed brighter, almost impossibly so, so bright that it hurt her eyes. She clutched her pilfered jar against her chest and began retracing her steps through the palace, moving as quickly as she dared. Someone could come around a corner or open a door at any moment, and dropping the jar could have much worse consequences than dropping a candle. What would happen if she smashed a jar that contained a still-human, still-beating heart?

Nothing good that she could think of. So Zib hurried, but not too fast, until she heard voices up ahead and ducked behind a corner, breathing too quickly.

Avery and the Queen of Swords.

The Queen was speaking in a low, warm tone, like the voice of a beloved babysitter, someone who could be trusted to be firm but kind, always up for another game, a willing co-conspirator within reasonable limits, a friend and a confidant. Zib, who knew none of these things were true reflections of the Queen, hated to hear it. It made her want to claw at her unnaturally whitened skin until the white ran red with blood, until she had done *something* to show that she was still the master of her own shape.

She didn't. The Queen had already done her enough harm. She didn't get to be commemorated with scars.

"—find them, we'll be able to sit down to a nice breakfast, all of us together, and share our dreams. Won't that be lovely? A breakfast is always better when shared with the people we care about. We walk our own worlds when we sleep, and every new day is a bright reunion."

"I never thought about sleep that way."

"No, you wouldn't have, would you? You're a child yet, and used to other people mapping your journeys. It won't be until you're older that you realize sometimes, the journeys you take entirely on your own are the most difficult and complicated of them all."

The voices were getting softer as they continued. They were moving away. Zib still pressed herself flat against the wall, trying to blend into her surroundings, until she was sure that she was alone. Once the voices had faded out entirely, she still didn't move, only closed her eyes and whispered, "Jack Daw, I need you now."

The palace was full of winds and little breezes, and Jack had said that they carried messages to him. She could only hope he'd hear her. So she asked the air, and then she stayed where she was, eyes closed, until she heard the sound of wings. They beat in the silence of the hall like the heart in her hands, and Zib opened her eyes to see a great dark flock of gray-capped birds whirling through the air in front of her, performing an elaborate aerial dance that somehow never stopped or stuttered, even when she was sure they must slam into one another.

The whirling mass grew denser and denser, birds moving closer and closer together, until there were no birds at all, could never have been any birds, only Jack Daw, standing there as casual and careless as ever, head cocked to the side as he gazed at her.

"Well?" he asked. "Did you find the place where the winds don't go?"

In answer, Zib handed him the jar.

Jack froze, eyes going wide as he stared at it. "Do you . . . do you know what this is?" he finally asked.

"It's a jar," said Zib. "There's a heart inside, but there's no name on the outside, and all the others had names. I thought it might belong to you."

"It does," said Jack, and opened the jar, and slid his hand inside, withdrawing it with a beating heart—*his* beating heart—cradled in his palm. He stared at the wayward organ, eyes still terribly wide. "I never thought I'd see this again."

"It wasn't hard to find," said Zib. "You could have found it for yourself, if you'd gone looking. I could even show you."

"I couldn't," said Jack, still staring at his heart. "No one who belongs to the Queen could. It's part of why we didn't wake your Crow Girl. Even if she'd tried to help, she couldn't have been the one to find where my mother was keeping what she'd taken."

"Ah," said Zib, and a small knot of worry unsnarled itself inside her. She'd been half-afraid, in a disconnected, uncommitted sort of way, that the theft of her color along with the exchange of her freckles—because no matter how upset she was, she couldn't quite bring herself around to calling her freckles *stolen*, not when she'd willingly offered them up in payment for their stay—had transformed her into one of the Queen's creatures, even if not completely. But look, here she was, finding what the Queen wanted concealed. She was still her own girl, and not the Queen's monster.

It was a good feeling.

"But you found it," said Jack. "You found my heart, and now I have it again, and I can stop belonging to her if I want to."

"My mother says I'll always be her little rabbit," said Zib.

"Is your mother a fox, set to pounce on you and gobble you up?" asked Jack.

Zib blinked before shaking her head. "No," she said. "Or at least, I don't think she is. I think she's just a mother, and everybody ought to have one, if they have the chance."

"Then you can be her little rabbit as long as you want to be," said Jack. "Not every mother is a beast, waiting to swallow and devour, but some of them are, and those are the ones who never learned the art of letting go. My mother has never let go of anything once she had hold of it, has kept every scrap and speck of every good thing she's ever been able to catch, and that includes me. She'd keep me for her own until I was old enough to be a father to my own chicks, keep me tied to her nest so that I could never fly away, no matter how much I wanted to, no matter how much I needed to. She'd keep me here forever. I don't want that."

"Oh," said Zib. Then: "If the Crow Girl doesn't remember her name since she gave it to the Queen, how can we know which heart is hers? Because there were so many. If she can't tell us which one she wants, how will we find it?"

"If you can take her where you found this, it will know her," said Jack. "Mine hasn't been with me since I was a baby, and it still knows me." He closed his hands around the heart, hiding it from view, then slipped it into his pocket.

Zib blinked. She had thought that somehow he would put the heart back into his chest, to beat like an ordinary heart did. She had also thought, on some level, that he'd been speaking metaphorically when he said the Queen of Swords had taken his heart away, because a person couldn't live without a heart to move their blood around inside their body, and he was very much alive. But then, a person couldn't burst into a flock of birds, either, and he did that as easily as breathing. So maybe metaphors didn't really happen here in the Up-and-Under. Maybe everything meant exactly what it said and said exactly what it meant, and she was just being slow to learn that lesson.

"Don't you want to put your heart back where it belongs?"

"No," said Jack. "My mother stole it from me when I was only a baby—and I do mean she *stole* it, because I was too young then to tell her she could have it. I think I would have given it willingly, if she'd waited until I was a little older. Most children will give their hearts to their mothers if asked, even if those mothers are ungenerous or cruel. The love of children for the ones who care for them is so strong that it overwhelms self-interest, no matter how selfish or greedy the child. But she didn't want to wait and risk her crown, and as strong as the love of children can be, the love of mothers is often stronger, and more consuming. We have no desire to devour our parents when we're small. They, on the other hand, always remember that we were born of them, and part of them wants back the flesh that we have taken without permission. Most parents are unable to give in to this wanting. Not so, my mother. She reached into the secret places inside me, and she took what was no longer hers to have, and she kept it away from me for all these years."

Zib listened, transfixed and horrified, and said nothing.

Jack looked at her, and he smiled. "So you see, I am older than you are, if not as old as she is, not quite a man grown, but close enough to such that I can see it when the clouds clear and the sun strikes the horizon, and I have done all my growing without the having of a heart. If you can find your Crow Girl's heart and restore it to her, it will help her to remember who she was before she gave it away. If I were to place my heart back inside my chest, it would remind me of what it was like to be an infant, helpless and defenseless and small, and all-consumed by the love of a mother who was willing to do me harm to serve her own desires. That Jack is behind me, and he never grew up. Let him stay in the cradle, let him learn what kind of monsters mothers can be, and let him be forgotten. I prefer to stay as I am, and if I am a little heartless, that's my decision."

"Can you never be yourself and have a heart?"

"Now that I have my original heart back in my keeping, it's possible that I might, with time, be able to grow a replacement," said Jack carefully. "I would need to find something worth caring about dearly enough to make a heart a worthwhile burden, but I think that could be accomplished. You've done what I needed from you, and what you needed from yourself. Go and find your Crow Girl, and take her to the hall of hearts. Her heart will know her, and she was old enough when she lost it to have known who she was and what she was doing. She can take it back again without losing herself completely."

"All right," said Zib, and moved to go. Jack grabbed her arm, stopping her.

"When you move to hand her back her heart, you must demand a single crow," he said, voice low and urgent. "You must take one of the birds she began with and hold it apart from the rest of her as she slides her heart back into place. That will keep the person she's become free from the rest of her."

"Then couldn't we keep one of your birds out and let you take your heart back?"

"I don't have any of my original birds left," said Jack, letting go of her arm. "I've been birds for so long that there's not a single feather left of what I started with. Once a flock has cycled completely, there's no getting back to who or what they were before, not without losing everything they've gained since breaking into pieces. Your Crow Girl is close to that point, but she hasn't crossed the line yet. Now go."

This time when Zib began to hurry away, he didn't stop her, only stood where he was and watched. Once she was gone, he pulled the heart from his pocket and looked at it for a long moment, eyes bright with longing. Then he returned it to its hidden space and burst like a balloon that had been filled with black-winged birds instead of air. They flew in all directions to begin with, but quickly settled to sweeping down the hall toward the nearest window, leaving the hall empty.

Zib hurried to retrace her steps, all too aware that she could run into Avery and the Queen, but less afraid of that possible encounter now that she was no longer carrying a stolen jar. And perhaps it was the absence of her fear that arranged things such that she encountered no obstacles until she had reached the last stairway between her and their rooms, where Niamh was sitting glumly on the top landing.

She looked up as Zib rushed past her, beginning to rise. "Zib!" she called. "Where have you been?"

"Where we both intended to be," said Zib, not wanting to name the place. With Jack standing there to cajole any eavesdropping winds into taking their side over the Queen's, it had been easy to be more open about her morning's adventure. Here and now, it seemed like the very height of foolishness to speak her destination aloud. "Have you seen the Crow Girl?"

"Not today," said Niamh, and followed her down the stairs, into the hall where the bedrooms were. "Did you find what we were looking for?"

"I did, and I heard Avery talking with the Queen of Swords, so I guess she found him," said Zib. The hall was empty. They hurried on to the door to the Crow Girl's room, where Zib stopped and knocked.

"She knows everything that happens in her palace," said Niamh.

"I know," said Zib. "I think Jack can keep some things from her, when he wants to, but he has to want to, and he doesn't want to do anything that doesn't at least amuse him."

Maybe he would be different now that he and his heart were together again, even if he never slipped it back into his chest. Was proximity to a heart enough to make it do the work a heart was meant to be doing?

Zib knocked again.

Niamh frowned. "She should be here by now," she said.

"Unless she's asleep." Zib knocked a third time, harder, until it felt like she was practically pounding on the door. When there was still no answer, her stomach sank, and she exchanged a sharp look with Niamh before opening the door to reveal a small room, almost identical to her own, save for the bed, which had been replaced by a giant nest of woven wicker, piled high with pillows.

The only sign of the Crow Girl was a handful of black feathers on the floor next to the open window. Zib crept forward, peering into the bed-nest. It was, as she had expected it to be, entirely empty.

Niamh leaned up next to her. "Maybe she's gone with the other Crow Girls to look for breakfast," she said.

"Maybe," agreed Zib glumly.

The door slammed behind them. Both girls whirled, guilty and grateful for the distraction in almost equal measure, and the Queen of Swords looked down her elegant nose at them, Avery by her side, her hand locked on his shoulder like she thought she could strangle even the idea of trying to run from her.

"Well, well," she said. "It seems our little bird has flown the coop, and now her little friends are looking for her. I wonder why. I wonder what naughty little game you could be planning to play that would need you to have her by your side."

Avery looked at the two of them, frantic and helpless, eyes very wide, and the light glinted off his skin. Zib realized to her horror that even as her color had been stolen away from her, his skin had been transformed into a hard, glittering substance, like a piece of pyrite as clear as glass and filled with faceted rainbows. He shone. Every time the light struck him, he shone.

"It's not your concern," said Zib stiffly, pulling herself up as tall as she could go. "We've paid our room and board for the day, and more than our room and board, since you stole more from me than I'd told you you could take, and that means the games we want to play are our own."

"About that," said the Queen, and dipped a hand into the pocket of her gown, pulling out a small bottle that Zib recognized hazily, as one might remember something only seen in a dream. "Your friend pointed out to me that our agreement had been for your freckles only, and not for the pigment all around them. You have my apologies for any distress you felt when you saw yourself and thought that I had overstepped my bounds."

She lobbed the bottle to Zib, underhand, so that it was easy for the girl to snatch it out of the air. Even stoppered, it smelled of lemons and roses.

The Queen of Swords smiled, indulgently. "The freckles are mine, of course; a deal's a deal, and as I've upheld my side of the bargain, there's no reason for me to return them. But the color of your skin is in there. Only drink it, and you'll be as you were. Minus the little specks and spots that I took fairly."

"What have you done to Avery?" asked Niamh.

"Nothing that he didn't consent to," said the Queen. "The freckles were good for a night's slumber and supper, as well as the following breakfast, which all you naughty children seem to have elected not to eat. That doesn't make it *free*, you understand; a cracked egg must be paid for if you don't want the farmer to starve, whether or not anyone comes to have it for their teatime. Your friend very cleverly realized that this meant my hospitality would be ending as soon as the clock struck lunch, and chose to pay your next day's stay."

"How can he go *home* like this?" blurted Zib.

"Boys aren't covered in glitter and rainbows where we come from!"

"Oh, my," said the Queen, sounding theatrically surprised. She turned to look Avery up and down, taking her time, as if she weren't looking at her own handiwork. "Why, I suppose that he can't go home like this, is the answer you're looking for." Her tone turned smug. "He'll have to stay here, in the Up-and-Under, and find a new normal for himself. And if he wants that normal to be here in the Land of Air, I'm sure we can find a place for such a quick and clever lad. If he doesn't, well. A little part of him will always be here with me, and he'll never be entirely earth again, no matter how far he roams."

"You don't just make monsters, you *are* a monster," said Zib.

"Maybe so," said the Queen of Swords, finally taking her hand off of Avery's shoulder. "Don't you want your color back? He argued dearly to return it to you."

Zib stared at the little bottle in her hand, and then at the Queen. "If I say no, does that change the terms of your deal with him?" she asked. She had learned the risks of agreeing too quickly, and of thinking first of herself, before she thought of anyone else. She didn't want to be a paper-person for the rest of her life, but she could carry a parasol and tell people she had a terribly unusual medical condition, if things came to that. She had *options*.

The way she saw things right now, that was more than Avery had.

"No, sadly for your hollow hopes," said the Queen. "He's a clever boy, but not clever enough to have something for nothing. Your accounts are distinct from one another. He said he wanted to shine when he first got here, remember? I only gave him what he wanted."

"She's telling the truth, Zib," said Avery. He looked down at his feet, where his shoes were still as dull as anything. "I did say I wanted to shine."

"You also said you wanted to go home," said Zib. "Don't you want to go home? Our parents are waiting for us!"

"Parents are very good at waiting," said the Queen of Swords.

A bird cawed from the open window. Zib looked toward the sound. A big black bird was sitting there, sunlight glinting off the gray feathers of its head. It met her eyes and bobbed its head, before gesturing toward the air outside with its beak.

"Avery, come over here," she said.

The Queen of Swords took her hand away. "Go on, go and play with your little friends," she said, voice indulgent.

Avery didn't wait for her to change her mind. He ducked away and ran across the room to Zib and Niamh. Each of them took one of his hands in her own, the three children looking at the Queen of Swords, who watched them like a predator who knows her next meal is guaranteed, a small smile on her face.

"Where do you think you're going to go?" she asked. "It's a long, long way down."

"We've gotten very good at falling," said Zib, and ran for the window, the bottle in one hand and Avery's hand in the other, pulling her friends in her wake.

When she got there, she didn't hesitate, but stepped up onto the windowsill and leapt. Avery, for his part, didn't let go, allowing her to drag him with her into the open air. Niamh was right behind, still holding onto Avery's hand.

The three children fell for perhaps twenty feet—far enough for Zib to start questioning whether she'd done the right thing by allowing herself to be guided by a jackdaw. Maybe Jack had been trying to say something else, and been stopped by the absence of a human voice? Maybe she had just jumped out a window and dragged everyone else with her for no good reason.

Well, that would be a silly way for their adventure to end, and somehow that made it feel all the more likely. Zib closed her eyes, hand slipping out of Avery's, and went limp, allowing the wind to take her.

The wind, and the sound of wings. Feathers brushed every exposed part of her as she stopped falling. Zib opened her eyes.

They were surrounded by birds, birds on every side, black-winged and gray-winged and even white and blue-winged, corvids of every kind forming a living cloud around them. No single bird could have been strong enough to support the weight of a single child, and even all of them together couldn't entirely halt their descent toward the ground: they were still falling, just so slowly now that it wasn't even quite a tumble. If they reached the bottom at this speed, it wouldn't hurt, or be enough to leave a bruise.

Zib looked wildly around the cloud of birds until her eyes fixed on a gray-topped jackdaw. "She'll never forgive you for this," she said, voice low and urgent.

The bird croaked with what managed to sound very much like casual unconcern.

Zib laughed. "But I guess you don't care. Can you get us back into the palace? We must have fallen several floors before you stopped us, and the Queen can't watch *every* window, can she?"

The jackdaw shook its head, and the cloud of wildly flapping birds changed direction, still dropping lower in the sky, but now moving sideways at the same time, angling the children toward the nearest balcony. It was a small, ornate thing, built around a high-corniced window that stood open to admit the morning air. It would be the perfect way to get back inside.

Avery was the first to be set down, settled to his

feet by a flock of mixed corvids that brushed their wings against his cheeks as they pulled away, cawing their farewells. Niamh was the second, and she shuddered and staggered away from the birds before they could bid her any avian farewells. She caught herself against the wall, still shuddering.

"I *hate* falling," she said.

"You didn't seem to mind it as much when we fell into the Saltwise Sea," said Avery.

"It's not falling when there's water on the landing end," said Niamh. "It's *diving*, and diving is altogether different. It's a proper occupation for a girl of the water. Please stop making me fall off of things. I would prefer not to." And she tugged her dress back into place with a decisive sniff, apparently considering the matter closed.

"This world seems to be very fond of dropping us off things," said Avery, dubiously. "I don't think I can promise that."

The birds set Zib to her feet and dispersed, leaving her with a jackdaw on one shoulder and a crow on the other. She turned first to the jackdaw.

"Thank you," she said, very seriously. "We were in a lot of trouble back there, and I think your mother was done with playing nice, if she was ever playing nice in the first place." She kissed the side of the black and gray bird's feathery head, and it lifted into the air with a sound of surprise, wings flapping wildly, before it settled back into place.

Pleased, Zib turned to the crow. "Are you a part of our Crow Girl?" she asked.

The crow croaked what sounded like confirmation. Zib nodded.

"Can you pull the rest of you together, please? I need to talk to you."

The crow croaked again, hopping down from Zib's shoulder and landing on the balcony. More crows began sailing back to them, crow after crow—but so many fewer than there had been when they first met her. They clustered together, black-feathered bodies pressed close, until with a ruffle of their wings, they weren't crows at all anymore, but a small child crouching there and looking up at her with wide, worried eyes.

"Did I do something wrong?" she asked. "Only, the Queen said all the other birds were flying, and it was a beautiful day and I was hungry, and I thought I could go for just a little while. But I didn't mean to do something wrong."

"No, you didn't do anything wrong," said Zib hastily. "You're doing great. But we found the place where the Queen of Swords keeps all the hearts she takes from her flocks, and Jack says that if we can get your heart back to you, you'll remember who you were, and if I keep one of the crows you've always had with you outside the flock when you put your heart back in, you'll remember who you are, so you won't have to lose anything."

The jackdaws came together in a swirl of black and gray birds that transformed into Jack Daw, who was looking solemnly at the Crow Girl. "She's right, fledgling," he said. "You can keep hold of yourself, and once you have a heart, it won't matter how many birds you lose or gain, you'll still know exactly who you are."

"But what if I became birds because I didn't *want* to be that person anymore?" asked the Crow Girl. "What if this just makes me into someone bad, or nasty, or mean?"

"You don't have to," said Avery, the light glittering off his skin as he stepped up next to Zib. "But if you don't, and you lose any more birds, I don't think you'll be the same person you are now. So you're going to be someone else either way."

"And one of those someones gets to remember us and be our friend," said Zib. "Will you let us get you back your heart?"

Looking uncertain, the Crow Girl nodded. "I guess if you think that's the best thing for me to do, that's probably the best thing for me to do," she said. "So yeah, okay."

"Then we move." Zib glanced to Jack. "Are you coming with us?"

"My mother's going to be furious when she realizes what you're doing," he said, lightly. "Of course I'm coming with you. Anything that makes her lose her temper is something I would very much like to see, and if she catches up to you—which she will—you'll want someone she isn't willing to harm."

He leaned over then, tucking a lock of hair behind the Crow Girl's ear.

"Besides, how could I leave this adorable fledgling alone with all you land-bound nimbies? She needs a proper flock to keep her safe, and as none of you saw fit to barter your heart for wings, I'm the only one she's got."

The Crow Girl giggled. All of them smiled, relieved to one degree or another, and as a group they moved through the balcony door into the small sitting room on the other side.

It was done up entirely in pink, rose, and palest orange, like stepping into a sunrise, and it was beautiful and it was ghoulish at the same time, because this wasn't the sort of room that could ever have been used for anything as casual or unimportant as *living*. Their feet hadn't touched the ground once since arriving in the palace, and yet it was impossible not to be convinced that they were tracking mud across the rosy carpet, besmirching the wallpaper with their very presence. They were a stain on this perfect place, and no one likes to feel as if they can contribute nothing to their surroundings, like they exist only to despoil.

They kept moving, following Jack out into the hall, where he turned and looked at Zib.

"You'll have to guide us from here, fire-girl," he said. "I don't know the way."

The others looked to her as well, expectant.

Zib squirmed. "I lost my candle," she said. "And we started from a different place in the palace before."

"I can tell you where your rooms are from here," said Jack. "Will that be good enough?"

"It might be," said Zib dubiously.

"Well, then, they're three stories above us, almost directly," said Jack. "Imagine you'd gone down three stairways, and you'd be here."

Zib paused in the hall, closing her eyes as she slowly turned a circle. Finally, she nodded, and started walking.

It was a slow progress, made slower by the fact that none of them wanted to speak, for fear that the Queen's winds would hear them and carry news of their location. Zib led, and the rest followed, down halls that looked half-familiar to her and entirely unfamiliar to her companions. Even Jack paused and looked around himself in confusion at times, clearly surprised by his surroundings.

Zib never varied her pace, neither hurrying nor dawdling, trying to retrace her steps without second-guessing herself. Another set of stairs down, another series of halls, and she was leading them directly toward a wall.

Niamh made an interrogative noise, eyebrows

raised. Zib looked at her and nodded, then reached out and touched the wall.

There was a pause, long enough to make them all—Zib included—wonder whether she had led them astray. Then, as before, the wall swung inward to reveal a dark hallway, and Zib stepped through. "This is where the winds don't go," she said. "We can talk here, I think."

"If we can't, we'll know it soon enough," said Jack, following her into the dark.

"There's stairs up ahead," said Zib. "We have to go down again. Come on."

The others followed her, feeling their way along the walls, the Crow Girl holding tight to the tail of Jack's shirt, her tiny hands shaking. Jack bent and scooped her into his arms, getting her off her feet, and thus carried her down the stairs as the group descended into the deeper darkness.

Once again, Zib opened the door to the narrow room lined with jars. Niamh gasped as she stepped inside.

"So *many*," she breathed. "I knew the Queen had been busy, but I never knew there had been so *many*. It seems like there must not be anything left of the world but monsters."

"There are no jars for the ones who had no names to steal," said Jack grimly, as the door swung shut behind them. "The bees and mice and little lizards who she twisted into great, terrible things, they needed less remaking to be transformed into her creatures. Only thinking things need to lose names and hearts to become completely hers."

"Which one of these is yours?" asked Zib, looking to the Crow Girl.

"I don't know," the Crow Girl whispered, unable to quite keep her eyes on Zib's face. Niamh nudged her in the ribs with her elbow.

"The Queen gave you back your color," she said. "Now might be a good time to put it where it belongs. You're a trifle unnerving to look at right now, and I think you're frightening her."

"Oh," said Zib, understanding. She pulled the cork from the bottle. The smell of lemons and roses wafted out. "I'm sorry. I didn't mean to scare you," she said, and drank the contents down in one long gulp.

They were sweet and slightly chalky, like the stomach medicine her mother sometimes brought home from the chemist. That thought sent an almost sickening wave of homesickness washing through her. She missed her home and her bed and her parents and yes, even her school, her teachers and her books and all the things she didn't know yet, but hoped she would someday. The Up-and-Under was a wonderful diversion, a mystery and a miracle, but as it seemed determined to kill them before they could grow up to be adults on their own, she wasn't sure how long she could safely stay here.

The Land of Air was keeping them from the improbable road. The improbable road was the only way they were going to find the Queen of Wands, and without her, they would never be able to properly access the Impossible City. The journey home began with a road and ended with a city, and she was more than ready to resume it.

Another wave of sickness crashed through her, and this time there was nothing of home about it. The bottle slipped from her fingers to clatter on the floor as Zib clutched her throat, coughing and choking. She sank slowly into a crouch, as Jack set the Crow Girl on her feet and bent to rub Zib's back with one hand.

"Hush, hush," he said, soothingly. "It's always easier to take something away than it is to give it back again. This isn't meant to do you harm, I promise. Just breathe through. You'll be on the other side soon."

Zib shot him a frantic look and kept on breathing, as the tightness in her chest loosened, as she found herself once again able to stand. She looked at her own hand, and breathed out in relief as she saw the ordinary beige of her fingers. She was the proper color for a Zib again, and not someone else's idea of what a little girl should be.

"Is that better?" she asked, of the Crow Girl.

The Crow Girl looked at her and sniffled, once more holding on to the tail of Jack's shirt for dear life. Zib smiled as encouragingly as she could.

"Look where we are," she said, and spread her hands. "This is where the Queen of Swords keeps all the things she steals away. Your heart is here. If you can find it, we can make sure we won't lose you. Do you know how to find your heart?"

The Crow Girl shook her head, eyes gone very wide and solemn. Zib, who also didn't know how to find a heart, looked helplessly to Jack. For his part, Jack only shrugged. His heart hadn't been hidden from him behind a shield forged from his name; of all the Queen's creatures, he had been left best equipped to recover himself whenever the need occurred to him.

"When someone who has lost their heart draws close to it, it will try to get back to them," said Niamh. The others turned to look at her. She shrugged. "I never lost my heart. The eel that ate it still rests in my chest, silent as a stone, heavy as an anchor. But I know the way hearts can function. Part of why I wanted to linger on the shore when my lake thawed was that if the people who lost me had come across me, my heart would have begun to beat again, even inside the eel. I would have felt it echo through my bones in the moment before my body realized that 'drowned' is another way of saying 'dead' and dropped me to the stony ground as a common corpse. Hearts always know. Hearts can't be fooled."

"But there are so many," said Avery. "She can't open them all."

"No," said Jack. "Mother would never leave us here for so long as that. We've slipped outside her seeing. She has to be looking for us already; she'll be here soon enough."

Zib looked at the floor, where her candle should have been, and gasped, the sound small and strained. The candle she had dropped was gone. The Queen of Swords knew that her private space had been violated.

"Hurry," she urged. "Jack's right. We don't have much time."

The Crow Girl looked at her and sniffled before she began walking along the shelves of hearts, allowing the tips of her fingers to trail over the surface of each jar as she passed it. There was silence, broken only by the rustle of her feather dress and the soft shushing sound of her skin rubbing across glass and porcelain.

Zib cast anxious glances at the door, waiting for it to slam open and the Queen of Swords to come striding inside. She didn't notice how the floor under their feet had started to gleam, taking on the nacreous shine of a sea snail's shell, not until Avery looked down and laughed from sheer delight. His skin was still sparkling brighter than the floor, and yet he seemed so overjoyed that it didn't matter.

"It found us!" he cried. "The improbable road, it finally found us!"

At the same moment, the Crow Girl stopped, staring at the jar under her fingers. "I can feel it," she whispered. "It's beating so hard it's like a whole flock crying out to the morning. This is mine." She reached up with both hands then, taking the jar down from the shelf, cupping it in her palms. "This belongs to me."

Jack took the jar out of her hands, and she didn't fight him, merely looked at him with wide and wounded eyes as he turned it over and looked at the back. "Soleil," he said. "Is that you?"

"I think so," said the Crow Girl. She reached for the jar. He ignored her, removing the lid.

"It's beating like anything," he said. "Do you want it?"

There was something weighty in that question. She paused, looking at him warily. "I think so," she said again.

"You won't be able to be quit of it a second time once you have it," he said. "Not without my mother's intervention."

"I'm sworn to the improbable road now, and I need all the pieces of me if I'm to walk it to the end."

"Then give Hepzibah one of your birds," he said.

The Crow Girl glanced, startled, to Zib. "One of my birds?"

"To hold the memory of who you've become in your days without a heart," he said. "Being heartless changes you. You can push those two selves together, but only if you keep them both alive long enough to try."

"All right," said the Crow Girl, and reached one hand into her own belly, pulling it out with a crow clutched in her fingers. It croaked and cawed, complaining about this rough treatment, and she planted a kiss atop its feathered head. "Go to Zib," she said, and let it go.

The crow flew straight to Zib and landed on her shoulder, ruffling its feathers as it settled. On the other side of the room, the Crow Girl gestured for Jack to give her the jar. He lowered it, and she snatched it away, sliding one hand inside and pulling out a beating heart that lit up from inside like an ember, glowing red and orange and rose. Unlike the Queen of Swords' sitting room, the colors were beautiful, perfect, and slightly blemished by the ashen crust around them.

"You're mine," said the Crow Girl to the heart in her palm.

The door slammed open, and the Queen of Swords practically fell into the room, taking in the scene in an instant, from the pearl-gleam of the floor and the crow on Zib's shoulder to the heart in the Crow Girl's hand.

"Put that down this instant, young lady," she snarled. "That doesn't *belong* to you!"

"No," said Jack. "But I'm your son, and you tell me all the time that everything that's yours is mine, except for the crown you stole from me when I was too small to tell you that you could. So her heart belongs to me, and I gift it to her now. Soleil, put it back where it belongs."

The Crow Girl nodded, short and tight, and pressed the burning heart to her chest, where it melted into her gown of feathers and disappeared.

The sound of wings came rushing down the hall behind the Queen of Swords. She stiffened, turning to close the door that she had left open upon bursting into the room, but it was already too late; an endless wave of black birds washed over her, crow after crow forcing themselves into the room. They swirled around the Crow Girl—around Soleil—who dropped the jar and burst into birds, joining the greater flock.

Niamh cried out, surprised and small, and Jack was there to steady her. "Don't be afraid," he said. "These are the birds without a murder to call their own. They come because they can hear her heart calling to them, and some crows do better with a heart to anchor them. This is normal."

The birds swirled. The Queen of Swords snarled, jabbing one sharp-tipped finger at each of the children in turn, beginning with Avery and ending with Jack.

"Betrayers," she spat. "Thieves. I give you hospitality—I give you a *home*—and this is how you would repay me? By touching and taking what isn't yours? How *dare* you. You don't *deserve* the Impossible City!"

"And you don't deserve us," said Jack. The vast knot of black-winged birds was still swirling in the center of the room, pressing tighter and tighter together, so that there was virtually no space left between them.

Then there were no birds at all, and only a tall teenage girl on the verge of womanhood, wearing the black feathered dress they all associated with the Crow Girls, blinking in the light as if such a thing had never once been seen before, as if this—all of this—were completely new. Her hair, still mostly black, was streaked with red, like seams of fire showing through coal.

She turned to the Queen of Swords, who winced and hung back, a sudden simpering smile on her face. "Soleil," she said. "What a pleasure to see you again. Why, we've missed you in these halls."

Soleil looked at the children around her with no hint of recognition, and frowned. "Where am I?" she asked, and her voice was the same and different at the same time, heavy with the weight of a life lived before bursting into birds, when she had been a woman named Soleil, and never walked the improbable road with a drowned girl and two children from the country of America. "How did I get here? Serafina, what is going *on*."

The Queen of Swords straightened and stepped toward her. "Terrible things," she said. "The boy beside you is my son, Jack, who has decided to raise up an army against my crown, and these children are members of his army. They cannot be trusted. They cannot be allowed to continue. But you and I, we have business to attend to, and I believe you owe me a heart."

"The bird, Zib," said Niamh sharply. "Send her the bird."

Zib scooped the crow from her shoulder and lobbed it lightly into the air, so that it beat its wings in surprise and hovered where it hung. "Go to Soleil," she said. "Go to our Crow Girl."

"No," snarled the Queen of Swords, and moved as if to snatch the crow out of the air. Jack snorted and broke into birds, mobbing his mother in a swirl of claws and talons, pecking and scratching at her as the crow winged toward Soleil, slamming into her chest just below where she had placed her heart.

Soleil gasped, bending forward. When she straightened again, her eyes were blazing, bright as embers, and twice as filled with fury. "I did not agree to what you did to me," she spat. "We made a bargain, you and I, and you took more than you were offered, and then, to give me to that—to that *man*, like I was a trinket or a toy to be traded away. How dare you? How *dare* you?"

The Queen of Swords winced, but gathered her composure and straightened. "I dared because you were never going to know," she said. "There was no possible way you were ever, ever going to know. I dared because it removed you from my path, and now you've set yourself back across it, an obstacle better left avoided."

"But we have a road to walk," said Jack, seizing Soleil's hand and tugging her toward him. "Come, children, wave goodbye to my mother, goodbye, Mother! And come along, for we have very far to travel yet."

Soleil looked, for a moment, like she was going to resist. Then she yielded, and turned, and the other children fell into step behind her, and the Queen of Swords could only stand and watch in silence as her guests, her monster, and her son walked away, and she was left behind.

EPILOGUE

BACK TO THE
IMPROBABLE ROAD

As it always seemed to do, the improbable road knew precisely where it wanted them to go. It led them out of the room and down another hallway to a door that led into a brightly lit ballroom with an open picture window at one end. The road unspooled from there, seeming to hang itself upon dust motes and air, becoming a glistening rainbow suspended in nothing at all.

Zib, who had become very good at falling, was the first to step out onto the soap bubble surface of the road, and smiled when it held her weight. "No foot-stomping this time," she said, to Soleil, who she still thought of as the Crow Girl, and probably always would. "All right?"

"All right," said Soleil, and stepped onto the road. The others followed the two of them, even Jack, who tucked his hands into his pockets and strolled nonchalantly onto the improbable road, which seemed to hesitate for a moment before it held him up.

"It seems I'm part of your merry band for now," he said. "Well, then, I suppose we should be moving, before Mother thinks to set her storms upon us."

And indeed, the horizon was beginning to blacken as the Queen's Page whipped the clouds into a frenzy.

"Can we be rained off the road?" asked Avery.

"I don't think so," said Niamh. "Unless we offend the road into abandoning us, I don't think we can be forced to leave it. I've never walked the improbable road through the sky, so I can't be completely sure, but it seems to me that as long as we keep moving, we'll be fine."

"We have to go now," said Zib abruptly.

"What?" asked Avery.

"You bartered with the Queen for another day of safety. Well, if she sets her storms on us, then we're actively *un*safe, and your deal is null and void. You can have back the skin you came here with, and then you can go home when all this is over."

"I want to go home," said Avery, and started walking.

All of them moved as quickly as they dared while walking on a thin rainbow above the distant ground. It was still going up, for that matter, and as they walked, it became apparent that the improbable road's solution to storms was to place their group above them, rising higher and higher under their feet, until they were walking over all but the very highest clouds. Zib couldn't look down without feeling her stomach flip and churn. She was getting remarkably good at falling, but this was a fall she couldn't even consider.

"Are you sorry?" asked Soleil, looking at Jack. He shook his head.

"No," he said. "Are you?"

"Maybe," she said, and they walked on, three children of the Up-and-Under and two children from another world, following a rainbow road across the sky, above and away from the storm-filled clouds, away from the palace of the Queen of Swords. They walked on, as the air warmed and the improbable road began dipping downward under their feet, toward the only destination left to them, toward the bright, burning country of fire.